PRAISE FOR *CLEAVE THE SPARROW*

GOLD BOOK AWARD WINNER. "Some books tell a story. Others drag you into a chaotic, unrelenting experience that scrambles your brain and leaves you questioning everything. *Cleave the Sparrow* is the latter. It's a fever dream wrapped in satire, political absurdity, existential horror, and bursts of unfiltered genius."—*Literary Titan*

STARRED REVIEW. "Aside from being the title of Jonathan Katz's uproariously funny, incredibly prescient novel, 'cleave the sparrow' is a Zen kōan, meant to enlighten spiritual students with its blunt and violent suggestion—devoid of all meaning except for that of the moment and of the action itself. Cleaving the sparrow is exactly what happens in the 300-some-odd pages of this extraordinary book."
—*Hollywood Book Reviews*

"There are books that challenge you, and then there's *Cleave the Sparrow*. With a narrative that feels like a fever dream engineered by a rogue AI, this novel is a stunning collision of political satire, psychedelic horror, and existential dread. It revels in its absurdity while dissecting profound truths about power, belief, and the fragility of perception. Daring, unpredictable, and utterly consuming, this is a novel that lingers in the mind long after you've closed the cover."
—*San Francisco Book Review*

FIVE STARS. "No summary can do this novel justice as its blend of surrealist humor, political satire, sci-fi, and philosophy made it the most unique book I've read in years."
—*Readers' Favorite*

"Successfully pushes satire to the absolute limit, and then some... Smacks of Burroughs, Burgess, and Philip K. Dick, with a good dash of Robert Anton Wilson."
— *The Independent Review of Books*

"At its core, *Cleave the Sparrow* is a novel about control—over perception, power, and reality itself. It's a book that weaponizes satire to peel back the layers of human delusion, from political theatrics to the very nature of existence. Wilder Crick's chaotic vision of the world is terrifyingly plausible, making this a story that is as intellectually provocative as it is disturbing. For those willing to question everything, this novel delivers a philosophical gut-punch unlike any other."
— *Chicago Book Review*

"In a narrative as mind-bending as it is darkly hilarious, *Cleave the Sparrow* dissects the illusion of reality with razor-sharp wit and philosophical depth. With a plot that spirals from political satire to metaphysical horror, the novel explores the futility of perception and the consequences of enlightenment. Every page brims with biting dialogue, psychological unraveling, and a cosmic punchline that lingers long after the final chapter. A brilliantly unsettling read that demands—and rewards—careful attention." — *Los Angeles Book Review*

"Gear up for a wild ride." — *Kirkus Reviews*

"To read Jonathan Katz's satirical novel *Cleave the Sparrow* is akin to being repeatedly struck on the funny bone: every laugh is accompanied by a wistful groan at the pickle the world finds itself in." — *IndieReader*

NOTABLE BOOK. "A truly moving ode with a keen sense of place that blends philosophy, elements of humor and science adroitly." —*Pacific Book Review*

"Creative and bitingly satirical… *Cleave the Sparrow* becomes something that, as its plot beats direct, transcends objective understanding in its self-awareness and distinctive choices." —*The Black List*

"Imagine a political thriller, a sci-fi mind-bender, and the weirdest cult documentary you've ever seen all mashed together, with a narrator who somehow makes existential horror laugh-out-loud funny. The characters are a mess (in the best way), and just when you think you know where it's going, it pulls the rug out from under you. If you like your books wild, smart, and just a little unhinged, this one's for you." —*Manhattan Book Review*

"A vigorous, edifying satirical novel." —*Clarion Reviews*

FIVE STARS. "Existential horror, political satire, and absurd comedy in perfect harmony, *Cleave the Sparrow* pulls readers out of their comfort zone into a realm demanding constant introspection." —*Chanticleer Book Reviews*

"A captivating, mind-bending ride… *Cleave the Sparrow* is raunchy, witty, incisive, and provocative. It reads like a mix of Chuck Palahniuk, Garth Ennis, and Neal Stephenson." —*BlueInk Reviews*

CLEAVE THE SPARROW

JONATHAN KATZ

CLEAVE THE SPARROW
(Author's Edition)

© 2025 Jonathan Katz

Published in the United States by Holofernes
An imprint of Holofernes Publishing Group ("Holofernes, LLC")
Printed in the United States
Cover design by Anze Ban Virant

ISBN: 979-8-218-65675-1
Library of Congress Control Number: 2025907353

For Sarah

CLEAVE THE SPARROW

I have a secret to share, little bird.

But my secret is difficult to hear,

and when you hear it,

a terrible battle will rage inside you,

and your senses will churn and roil,

and you will not survive it.

political
suicide

1

WE'RE IN THE SOUP.

T minus ninety-six hours, and he's down like a hotel comforter. Shelly walks in with the new numbers—even worse. Single digits in places. We're cooked. There's no coming back from this.

— Okay, she says.

— Okay, what?

— So, we're out of options. He'll have to debate. Go straight to the American people.

— But Shelly, he hates the American people—

— Only men, children, and seniors.

— He'll say awful things up there. He won't prep for it. They'll ask about his Nazi wardrobe—

— Two blazers and a tie clip is hardly a *wardrobe*, Tom.

— They'll ask about romancing the Espressolux. And he'll talk about it. He's weirdly proud of it—

— Hon, listen to me. What happens if we lose this thing on Tuesday?

— Armageddon, I know, but—

— And what happens if you and I just sit here on our hands for four days?

— I know, but—

— But?

I pause to give my next words the seriousness they deserve.

— He's fucking a coffee machine, Shel.

SHE'S RIGHT, OF COURSE. Shelly's smarter, better looking than me, she smells fantastic, and she really understands The Cause—I mean the actual science part, which gets a little confusing when you hit the tetrachromats. And granted, I'm not a scientist by any stretch, but I've heard our sales pitch about a hundred times for donors, New Party bigwigs, et cetera, and it goes like this:

What color is the sky, I ask you.

Well, Tom, it's blue, you say to me, and I say: Come on now, you can do better than that. All the great apes, I explain to you, have three different types of cone cells in their eyes, which means you and I can see about a million different colors—hundreds of thousands of shades of blue—only we're too lazy to make names for all of them. But if we ever did have names for every color and the time to study each one, then you could turn and say to me: Tom, the sky today is obviously Blue 89461.

Now some of you apes, about 2% of you, have only two types of cone cells in your eyes. So you can only discern about ten thousand different colors, or a tiny fraction of what the rest of us can see. In other words, you're screwed. You simply don't have the physical hardware you'd need to see the true nature of Blue 89461, and yet you'll still agree the color of the sky today is Blue 89461, because Blue 89461 doesn't actually *mean* anything. It's just the name we all gave to whatever we saw when we looked up at the sky.

You with me so far?

Because now along come these tetrachromats with four different types of cone cells. This is all true by the way. And these assholes, they can see about a hundred million different colors, including the *actual* true nature of Blue 89461, which turns out to be a color so mesmerizing and otherworldly, you and I would fall to our knees and piss blood if we caught even a glimpse of it, which of course we never can.

So now a few years go by, and the tetrachromats have taken over, and they're just about to start rounding us up and putting us in re-coloration camps or something, when this big spaceship lands, and out pops an alien slug with like a hundred trillion types of cone cells in its eyes—just an unfathomable number of cone cell variations.

And the leader of the tetrachromats knows he's beaten.

He bows his head and implores the slug king: Your majesty, please. I beg of you. Tell us, oh mighty one, what is it you see when you look up at the sky with your trillions of magnificent cone cells? And the slug king says: Oh, you'll never get anywhere with those.

— SHELLY FILLED YOU IN, TOM—about the new plan, the Hail Mary?

I nod, silently. He has an overbearing presence, our dear leader, so I try to keep quiet when he's around.

— Hard not to see it as defeat, he admits, but I suppose we all have a cross to bear, and you more than most.

He sees my posture stiffen, can tell I'm nervous.

— Tom, he says more gently now, do you even know why I chose you for this?

I shake my head.

— *That's why*, Tom. Because you'd never even think to ask. It's remarkable really. You're a true soldier. A true believer. And now here's the critical piece. I'll need you to follow some instructions of mine to the letter. *To the letter*, Tom.

I nod.

— People will try to talk you out of it. And you'll be incredibly tempted to use your own judgment. I need you to smother those instincts in the cradle, Tom.

Shelly pulls us aside.

— It's time.

She hands him his debate materials: a notepad, a ballpoint pen, and what appears to be a loaded .38 Special. Then Shel and I head to the green room to watch it all unfold on the jumbo monitors. On the left, the debate stage. On the right, our focus group of debate watchers, wired to the hilt with electrodes. One of Shel's people is in there with them, explaining how we're tracing their biological feedback and running it through our algorithm, and how feedback-based central node reset events or "brainquakes" are extremely uncommon these days.

— You look more nervous than they do, Shel says to me, and they're about to get electrocuted.

— I'm fine, really.

We can see Brent Crisswood on the left monitor now. Pompous shill. Over a hundred million eyeballs on him if you count the networks and the streamers. Just a handful of minutes left to save all our skins from total Armageddon.

— Good evening, ladies and gentlemen, says Brent. We've got an unexpected treat here tonight, a real honest-to-

God debate if you can believe it. First one in years, which means someone out there is feeling pre—tty damn desperate, am I right?

— Cocksucker, Shel whispers over the braying masses.

— Now then, says Brent, quieting the room, let's welcome to the stage our two candidates. First but not least, on my left, the current and God-willing future President of the United States, incandescent star of our beloved Demopublican Majority, author of the Kiev Accords, father of the Great Detente, mother of dragons—probably, overseer of eight glorious years of peace and prosperity, your hero and mine, President John D. Rockefeller Kennedy-Onassis Hemsworth the Third, Esquire. And on my right, I don't know, some irrelevant lunatic from the so-called New Party, Crib or something.

— It's Crick.

— Whatever, says Brent.

— Probably could have negotiated a better intro, Shelly admits.

She's not much of a strategist, Shel, but her hair smells incredible.

— Is that makeup, I whisper. He looks a little less green tonight than usual.

She nods, proudly. This is likely the first time most voters have seen Crick's face, and flesh-colored always polls better than the alternative.

— All right, says Brent. Let's begin. Now I want to ask mostly policy questions tonight, but there are a few — oh let's call them personal odds and ends we should address right off the bat. One of you seems to be wearing — is that a swastika tie clip, Crick?

— Remarkable man, Hitler. Took some impressive swings. Not all of them home runs, I'll concede it, but you've got to admire the sheer size of those Bavarian snow globes.

— Oh Brent, says the President warmly, can I chime in for a moment? I just want to reassure voters there's no admiration for Hitler in *our party*. And certainly none for his genitals, which I've heard on good authority were nothing to write home about.

— Typical politician's answer, says Crick. Poll-tested, no doubt.

The first focus group numbers flash across the right monitor. We're losing every demographic.

— And let me also note, adds the President, the only Bavarian snow globes I favor are the ones we place around der Tannenbaum at Christmastime.

— This fucking guy, says Crick.

— Now the other controversy, resumes Brent Crisswood, is a bit of a delicate matter as well. Is it true, Mr. Crick, that you've been shall-we-say romantically involved with a cappuccino machine?

— Just the milk frother, Brent, but I won't lie to you. It's an intensely erotic courtship. Suffice it to say I've voided a bit more than the warranty, if you catch my drift, you old dog.

— Oh Brent, says the President, just popping in here once more to remind voters there's been no hideous perversion of the natural laws in *our party*. And certainly not with a kitchen appliance, which doesn't seem entirely hygienic.

This isn't going well. The latest focus group numbers flash across the right monitor, and we're close to zero. There's only one bullet left in the chamber: Hail Mary full of grace.

— Let's get into your politics, says Brent. Mr. President, your platform calls for increasing military and social spending by 35% each, with bold new investments in energy and infrastructure. On the contrary, Mr. Crick, your proposal would eliminate *every* government program we have, diverting the entirety of our budget to a single line item called "special projects engineering." What exactly does that mean, sir?

— Well you see, says Crick in his favorite condescending tone, none of the people or the things you perceive in this world have any value to me because they don't exist in objective reality.

— Come again, says the President.

— We can't see the true nature of reality, any of us, Crick explains. Our eyes don't work that way. We've evolved to see what we need to see to survive, nothing more. This is scientifically proven, you understand. Everything you perceive—it's as Plato said, a bunch of shadows projected on a cave wall. So, what I'd like to do, you see, is take all our federal money, and use it to finally, *finally* blow up that fucking cave.

Some murmurs of confusion from the audience. This is probably the first time they've heard our actual pitch.

— Am I understanding, asks the President with utmost diplomacy, that the crux of the New Party's platform is an attempt to blow up the Earth?

— Appreciate the question, says Crick, which reveals with great efficiency the depths of your ignorance. Clearly, we'll need to blow up the cosmic projector that *manifests* the Earth, which is precisely what my tech delivers. But it's expensive—$7 trillion for the prototype, hence my need for high office and this humiliating grovel of a debate. Can I ask *you* a question now?

— Direct questioning is against the rules, says Brent.

He seems bored. I don't think he's been listening very attentively.

— What is it you actually believe in, Mr. President, asks Crick.

— Why I believe in the apple-cheeked goodness of American children, he says.

The audience erupts in spontaneous applause, some tears.

— But, in fact, you don't believe in anything of the sort, do you? I mean, not with any real conviction. I'm telling you that none of it—this podium, this town, your fruity children— none of it exists in objective reality, and you're telling me I'm wrong. But how *much* are you willing to risk, personally, to prove it?

The President stumbles, just momentarily. He's had no training for this. No poll-tested quips on Hitler's genitals at the ready.

— Look, Crick resumes, turning squarely to the audience. It's very simple. You all despise me—I understand that. You don't like the things I say. You're disgusted by my lizard-like appearance—

— Again, really good call on the makeup, Shel, I whisper.

— None of it makes a cunt hair's difference to me, he continues, because I've got something you deadheads simply can't resist. I'm going to tell you the future.

The crowd falls silent, confused, entranced.

— And I'm going to risk *everything* I have tonight—my own life in fact—to prove the accuracy of my predictions. So here it goes. Three little things. Three little things that cannot be prevented. Are you ready for it? Number one, I'm going to shoot myself in the face with this .38 Special revolver. Right here, right now. Should've discussed this with the cleaning crew, probably, but it's a hell of a closing argument, don't you think?

Brent is getting some sort of message from the control room in his ear, probably telling him to stop the debate for God's sake or maybe just to bypass the commercial break.

— Number two, in the wake of my gruesome expiration, you're going to elect my protégé to the office of the president. He's a good lad, Tom, unremarkable in all the right ways. You won't mind him. He's going to build my Earth-manifestation-piercing technology, and he'll get a good deal on it for you taxpayers who care about that sort of thing, which you really shouldn't because you don't exist.

A show of Secret Service deterrence now creeps into view on the fringe of the left monitor.

— Number three, he's going to blow up the cave and reveal the true nature of reality, at which point I'll return and take my rightful place on the throne of the universe.

Crick now brings the revolver dramatically up to his temple.

— Physical props are against the rules, says Brent halfheartedly.

He's definitely not paying attention.

— Now Crick, let's talk about this, says the President with a dignified but rising level of concern. You've got so much to live for, friend. How about a Cabinet position? Would that make you happy?

— The Cabinet isn't real, you dimwit. No, I shouldn't be surprised. Performative violence is all you troglodytes can understand. So, we'll do it that way.

Shelly holds her breath in anticipation, and I'm feeling suddenly lightheaded. There's sweat pouring down my face now. I'm not ready for the fallout.

— Pull the trigger, whispers Shel, as if willing him through the monitor, and a ferocious crack echoes across the stage as time collapses inward.

THUNK!

Brent startles upright, wiping blood spatter from his glasses.

Crick is dead.

No one speaks. For a minute, no one remembers how to speak. No one moves. No feeling at all beyond the tingling reverberations of the gunshot.

No light in the distance. No hope for the future.

AND THEN, when all seems lost and Armageddon assured, it happens—the miracle—just as Crick predicted it would. Some of the focus group lines start to tick a bit higher on the right monitor.

Then a lot higher.

Then a zigzagging pattern, which Shel later explains was a near-fatal brainquake in one of the volunteers.

Four days later I'm sipping bourbon in the Oval Office, because this is truly the strangest country on the face of the manifestation of Earth.

kill or
be kind

2

I'LL BET YOU'RE CONFUSED.

About Crick and the New Party, sure. But what I really mean is the confusion in your own life—your day-to-day existence. It's a feeling of estrangement, am I right? A nagging sense of loneliness and loss.

I can help with that.

One obstacle, though, is that you haven't seen what I've seen, which is sort of the whole point of the tetrachromats. And it's ugly what I've seen: the most intense of human suffering and the purest of all joys, which is the end of that suffering—or what my old mentor the Stonefish used to call the black/white illusion.

But you don't know about the black/white illusion, and you don't know about the Stonefish, which is why we'll need to backtrack for a moment. Although, now that I think on it, you've probably had *glimpses*.

Like when you've just finished the burrito más grande at Tacos Rojas, and you said you wouldn't eat the whole thing, but then you did anyway, and now it isn't sitting quite right, and you get this sudden flash of existential dread, because you've made a lot of poor decisions in your life and mostly skated past, but now you sense a terrible, final reckoning is upon you, and sure enough your insides start to twist and billow, and it feels like your spleen is getting squeezed in a combustion engine, so you rush home to the bathroom, and now you're sitting there, straining on the toilet, expelling pure foulness from both sides of the human equator, and it hurts to just exist in that moment, to breathe in and out, and you ask yourself why you aren't blacking out from this, because isn't your brain supposed to spare you from this type of extreme suffering, like when you lose a limb and your body goes into shock, which must mean that limb loss is even worse than spleen combustion, and now your consciousness is waning, and you can feel the blood draining mercifully from your cortex, and with your last bit of awareness you crawl off the toilet seat and into the bathtub, you know just to cover your bases, and when you wake up minutes later you feel a small tinge of relief, because the worst has crested, and the way down is a lesser pain, a sweeter pain by comparison, and it gives way to the numbness and stillness you've been craving, and you can even bear to stand after a while, and to clean yourself off and maybe run the bathtub for a minute as a general courtesy, and as you stumble out of the bathroom and collapse onto your soft, clean mattress, there's a feeling of indescribable bliss that overtakes you, because it's over, it's over, it's over, and you made it, for God's sake, you made it. Has that ever happened to you? You should probably go to a doctor if it keeps happening.

HERE'S ANOTHER WAY to look at it.

"Horror" these days is big business—books, movies, immersive experiences. And you can say we only enjoy these things because we know they're not real, but that isn't quite right.

When horror feels fake, it's no fun. So we seek out stories and experiences that seem more and more realistic—more and more visceral and harrowing. And if you follow this path to its logical end, you get to the Howitzer House in Deblaine, Tennessee. Do you remember that whole scandal?

Back when it happened, I was working for the local paper in Somerset. My editor said: Tom, you should go out there to the farm and do a lifestyle piece on Eugene Howitzer. You know, find out what makes him tick.

And this was before the scandal broke, so folks didn't know too much about him yet or what he was doing out there in Deblaine. Almost no one knew that the original Howitzer House was in Dumphry, Massachusetts, next to a Dunkin Donuts, until the city council shut it down after two weeks of non-stop complaints. So Eugene headed south and bought a hundred acres of Tennessee dirt farm, plus the parcels on both sides so there weren't any neighbors to complain about the screams. And in Deblaine, the sheriff said: We don't really care what you're doing out here as long as no one turns up dead.

SO, I'M ON ASSIGNMENT in Deblaine, right?

I get to the farm around ten o'clock, and it's pretty dark out there at night, but Eugene is hard to miss—a burly rectangle in full body armor.

— Welcome to Hell, he says with a chuckle.

— You mind if I tape record this, I ask him.

— I record everything, says Eugene. Everything we do out here, dude. It's the only reason I'm not in jail yet.

— You feel like you're being persecuted?

He grunts, and there's a sting to it.

— Folks just don't understand.

— Help me understand.

He grunts again, a little softer now.

— All right then. Think about the worst thing you've ever experienced.

— That's easy, I say, taking a quick mental lap through the intersection of burrito lane and bathtub boulevard.

— Now imagine something a hundred times worse than that, he says. Psychological pain so diabolical, so personal and vivid, it leaves a hole in your brain. I've had Marines in here. Navy SEALS, dude. When I'm done, they're empty shells of men. It takes me a month to plan this shit. I spend a *month* researching each person before they come through here, learning how to get inside their head.

— You'll have to show me what it's like.

He grunts again, this time with amusement. I guess if Navy SEALs can't handle the horror, it doesn't bode too well for English majors with a tree nut allergy. Also, I'm on deadline and don't really have a month to wait around while Eugene studies up on my old Slovakian babysitter with the removable teeth.

— What if I just talk to someone who's already done it?

— Much better plan, he says and writes a phone number on the back of a napkin. Be careful with her, though. She's a killer.

SHELLY'S BARELY TWENTY when we first meet up, and I wasn't careful at all. We agreed to have coffee at her apartment the next day, and she came to the door in a towel, and that was pretty much it.

— You're early, she says.

— I can come back later—

— Is it bad? I have nicer towels.

I'm thirty-six, you understand, and I've never had a girlfriend. Never kissed a girl. Never held someone's hand. And here's this absolute bombshell, teasing me, flirting with me even. And you wonder why people join cults?

— I'd feel better if you put on some clothes.

— Sexual hang-ups, got it.

She closes the door to her bedroom and leaves me in the hall. I take a look around—it's mostly empty. A few books, some liquor bottles. Moving in or moving out is my guess.

— It's depressing, I know, she says.

She's fully clothed now, but she's smoking an enormous joint.

— Might be better if we're sober for this, I say.

— Oh hon, I haven't been sober since—when was the robot president, she asks, taking a long drag on the roach.

— Twelve years ago.

— That was a weird time, though. Everyone was getting high.

— Would you say you have an appetite for self-harm, I ask her.

— It's more like I'm trapped in a cycle. Craving, pain, release. That's the cycle. Like when I shoot up heroin, and then I have to masturbate for days on end.

We make terrifying eye contact for a split second.

— Err—let's talk about the Howitzer House, I say, retreating from her gaze.

— Gene wouldn't give you anything?

— Nope.

— You're not really his type, she says. Let me see then. Okay, well, I guess what happens first is he makes you sign a waiver. And it takes a couple hours. Thirty pages of this fucking thing. I'm not even joking. He makes you read every word out loud, and he videotapes it. And all the while, he's saying things like: Look, you really don't want to do this. What's the matter with you, anyway? We're gonna break your brain, et cetera, et cetera.

— And none of that gave you any pause?

— You kidding? It was awesome.

— Fine, so what about afterward?

— After the waiver signing, he makes you wait for a while, alone, by the side of the road.

— Why?

— I dunno, atmosphere? Eventually, a van pulls up, and these two guys get out. They're dressed like paramilitary or something. They throw a bag over my head, duct-tape it around my eyes, and they toss me in the back of the van. Roughly, so I'll know they don't give a shit. Then I guess we're driving out to the farm. I can't see anything through the bag.

But the van stops after a bit, they pull me out, and they shove me into a room inside the house, and I wait there for another hour or so.

— What happens then?

— Then the lights come on, the tape comes off, the bag comes off my head, and Gene is standing over me with his video camera. We're alone, and he says: Look, I know you think I've got this diabolical mindfuck planned out, but really I'm just gonna beat the shit out of you, and if that doesn't work, I'm gonna drown you in a tank, and if that doesn't work, I'm gonna rape you. And there's no safe word for any of it. It's gonna happen no matter what you say or do, and it's gonna happen until either I decide you've had enough, or you die. And then he does it, and that's what happens.

— He raped you?

— No, we only ever made it to the tank.

— But he *would* have?

— I don't know.

— And that doesn't—I mean, jeez—it doesn't bother you at all?

— It scares me, which is what I asked him to do. Craving, pain, release, she says and blows a plume of pot smoke in my eyes.

— Here's what I'm trying to understand, I tell her, my eyes watering a little from the smoke. What was in your past?

Like, when he did his month of research into your history, what did he find there that led to this?

— He doesn't do any fucking research, she laughs. It's the same shit for everyone. Laziest motherfucker I ever met.

AFTER THEY PUBLISHED the story, Eugene got into some hot water with the Tennessee State Police. He never actually raped any Navy SEALs as far as I know, but he sent lewd videos and texts to a dozen of the women he tortured, and one of them was under eighteen. Also, it turns out that legally, you can't have people sign a waiver that indemnifies you from causing physical harm. It's just not enforceable. So a couple of the women sued, and Eugene got run out of town. They tore down Howitzer House brick by brick. Someone said they salted the earth after that. I mean, people *really* hated that place.

But not Shelly.

She was a satisfied customer to the end. More than that, even. I think she felt a little sad for Eugene and how it all turned out, as if he'd been providing an important public service that the world just couldn't understand.

A couple months after my story ran, I got a call from her, out of the blue. We hadn't spoken since the interview.

— Can I tell you a secret, she says. The universe is dying. I want you to write about it.

— That's not really my beat, Shel.

An awkward silence envelops us. Any rapport we once had is long gone, if it ever existed.

— Err—you want to meet at your apartment again, I ask to fill the quiet.

— No, I don't live there anymore. I was hoping you'd be up for some light travel.

— Yeah, all right.

— I'll text you the directions then. Dress warm. It's cold as shit in these dorms. See ya, bye—

— Shel, before you go, I—

— What now, Tom?

— I just don't understand it, still—why anyone would seek out these self-destructive things. It's not normal. Howitzer House. Heroin. Craving, pain, release.

— But you already know the answer, she says. It's why you're coming with me. Because we're the same like that.

— No, I—why would you say that?

— How real are we gonna get here, she asks.

— All the way.

— You're a fucking loser, Tom. Like, look at me, and look at you. It's never gonna happen with us, you must know that. But you're gonna follow me around like a lost puppy. Most men do it. You can't help yourself.

— That's not true—

— You know women can size-up potential mates in less than a tenth of a second? You know how that's possible—because it's not a goddamn analysis. It's just biochemistry. There's no love story for us. You're always gonna want that, and it's never gonna happen. It doesn't matter what you do. That's your heroin, Tom. That's your heroin.

I'm getting angry now, and I rarely get angry with anyone.

— You barely know me, I fire back at her. It's absurd. I hardly spoke to you. We met one time. You can't judge a person like that.

— Normally, I'd agree, she says. But you haven't seen what I've seen.

AND HERE'S THE THING about the tetrachromats I forgot to mention. They don't know they're any different. They just see what they see, as we all do, when they look up at the sky. And you can never *really* know a thing until you stand apart from it—until you've seen it from the outside.

So I swallowed up my pride and took the trip, which wasn't exactly as advertised, either. "Some light travel" was a three-day tour of the western Pacific Ocean. And those "cold-as-shit dorms" were an artery of subterranean caves.

I wasn't mad, though. Truth is, I'd have followed her to the ends of the earth if she'd asked me. All because I saw her in a towel once, which is proof enough I guess that we were doomed from the start.

But as my old mentor the Stonefish once said, there's only two ways to live this life—open or closed. Open yourself up, and pretty soon you're waiting in a van outside Howitzer House, with a bag on your head, duct tape over your eyes, and an unenforceable waiver in your pocket. You know it's going to hurt like hell, but you always finish the burrito.

tell it to the
machine elves

3

ALL MODERN SCIENTIFIC observation suggests our universe is dying.

Low-mass stars like our Sun, depleted of their nuclear fuel, will fade to dimming white dwarfs, then stagnant black dwarfs with no significant light or heat. High-mass stars will core-collapse into black holes, then evaporate as Hawking radiation. In the end, nothing will remain but the cold, dead uniformity of space.

Oh, but we've got loads of time before that happens, Tom, you say to me, and I say: Yes, I know it *feels* that way.

But if you listen to the scientists—if you believe, as Einstein did, that spacetime is a four-dimensional block, and our perception of time "passing" is a subjective mental illusion—then you'll find our slow-burn Armageddon is already here.

And unless we take corrective action in the present moment—like right this actual, literal second—our whole universe is doomed. That's according to Wilder Crick, a man whose televised execution dethroned the Queen Elizabeth sex tape as YouTube's most-watched video clip, and whose unpublished autobiography, *Everyone's Wrong But Me*, sits neatly at the edge of the Resolute desk in my new office.

But we're still not there yet.

I MET CRICK for the first time in Heilongjiang, China, in a subterranean cave.

He was living there with Shelly and three others, and I'll do my best to describe them.

First, there's a woman we called the Stonefish. Small and frail, she was. Maybe a hundred and forty years old, give or take a decade. Dressed entirely in animal skins, which isn't a bad way to go when you're deep underneath the frozen tundra.

Then there's Usama Quereshi, who we called Ravi back then. Crick's bodyguard—former Indian military. Tall, buff, extremely good looking.

And the third: a young boy, maybe ten years old, an American kid. And we called him Dr. Grace.

— Let's bite his dick off, says that little asshole the minute I set foot inside the cave.

He's naked except for a loin cloth. He has a massive, bulging forehead, black teeth, and a noticeable tremor, like he's tweaking on something.

— Don't mind the doc, says Ravi. He runs a little hot. You'll get the same welcome we all did—the drinking of the sacred brew.

— I'm just here to write an article, I tell him. Is Shelly around?

— I'll cut your dick off while you sleep, Grace whispers in my ear as he scuttles past me in the dark.

— Um—

— Everyone drinks the sacred brew, says Ravi. Shelly must have told you that.

— She didn't really go into details. For example, I sort of assumed we'd be closer to the Earth's crust.

— I'll peel the skin off your dick, Grace whispers, crossing back in front of me somehow.

— What is happening here, I yell in a higher pitch than intended. I want to see Shelly. I've come a *really* long way for her.

— The one you call Shelly does not exist, says the Stonefish.

Her voice is deep and sonorous, reflecting off the cave walls as she steps forward into the light. There's a roar of thunder in the distance.

— No, she does. We texted earlier, I say.

— I'll cut your dick into slices and eat the slices—

— Can someone take him for a minute?

— Once upon a time, says the Stonefish in a breathy baritone, we wanted to understand the body. To control it better. So we chopped it up into pieces—head, neck, shoulders. There's a pain somewhere in my body. To soothe it, I have to find it. So I create the fiction of a neck—a thing that's separate from the rest of me. Now I can better control the pain, because I can isolate it. But that act of isolation has a cost. I now believe, falsely, that the head is not the neck. That the body is not the air or the sunlight that sustains it. That the one you call Shelly is not the one you call Tom.

— So she's outside, or what?

— This will all make more sense, says Ravi, once you've had the sacred brew.

SHELLY TURNS UP about eight hours later, a little before sunrise. I haven't slept a wink because Dr. Grace has been sitting across from me all night, stroking a dagger.

— He runs a little hot, says Shel. I mean that literally. His resting body temperature is like a hundred and twelve degrees.

— Is that why he's so mean?

— He has a rare genetic mutation, says Crick, who must have slipped in behind her. His subcortical brain structures are extraordinary. Practically overflowing with the 5-H2TA serotonin receptors that bind to the dimethyltryptamine in our sacred brew.

— What?

— He can talk to the machine elves, says Shel.

— *What?*

— You must be Tom, says our dear leader, stepping into view as he lights a small fire in the corner of the cave. Wilder Crick's the name. Make sure you spell that right in the book.

— Err—Shelly, I say in the hushed voice one uses when first noticing the green, reptilian skin of a new acquaintance. Is this—I mean—is *he*—

— We're not fucking, Tom, if that's what you're asking, she says.

— Wasn't what I was asking—

— Time is a block, my dear. We might be fucking but you haven't realized it yet.

— Can we change the subject, I ask.

— Here's the thing about that, says Crick while placing a metal cauldron on the fire. You can't change anything, because you don't exist.

This is the point where I snap.

My patience for their nonsense has all but depleted, not to mention I'm exhausted from no sleep and seven hours in a rickshaw, which I was actually pulling for most of the trip while my driver took a personal call.

— I'm done. You're all nuts. Shel, best of luck with — yeah, whatever this is.

She looks at me with something new in her eyes. Is it grudging respect?

— Don't go, she says. Tom, you're about to join The Cause. It's the most important work you'll ever do. And while you've been lounging here all night, we were out in the freezing cold, schlepping supplies for your initiation. So maybe a little less attitude, shit head.

— C-R-I-C-K, says Crick. As in Francis Harry Compton, my great grandfather. Put that in the book as well.

Shelly slips away, deeper into the cave system. I stare at my feet, hoping Crick and I won't have to make much conversation.

— I sense a deep sadness in you, Tom, he says.

— I'm fine.

— Wouldn't be here if you were.

I open my mouth to object, but it's a roundly irrefutable point.

— Say, are you a religious man?

— Not really, I tell him. I was Catholic growing up.

— That's the one with snake handlers?

— I don't think — err — well, maybe up in the mountains?

— One thing I've learned from the Stonefish, he says, it's really all the same story. Eastern religion, Western religion, Northern — you know, Eskimo things.

— Is she some kind of guru then?

— She's seen everything there is to see. Grew up during the Han Dynasty.

I nod politely, but this is pretty hard to believe. I mean the woman is old, no question, but I wouldn't have guessed pre-Christ.

— Why do you call her that, the Stonefish?

— Technically, she doesn't have a name. But we had to put something down on the chore wheel, yeah? Deadliest fish in the sea, the stonefish, doling out the most painful sting of any animal on Earth. Nothing stings like the truth, am I right, Tom?

I shrug it off, but my last phone call with Shelly still echoes, faintly.

— So you're the leader of a cult?

— I don't like that word. Makes it sound like we're just out here serving poison to each other. And we are doing that, he says pointing to the cauldron, but it's not the whole syllabus.

— Curtains up, says Shelly, returning to the front of the cave with Ravi, Dr. Grace, and the Stonefish in tow.

The five of them take their seats in a circle around the fire.

— Stand before us, says the Stonefish.

— You are here, Initiate, says Crick, at the urging of our dear sister Shelly. Frankly the rest of us don't really see it, but I guess that's water under the bridge.

Ravi and the Stonefish nod their heads. Dr. Grace strokes a dagger.

— However, Crick warns, your place among us is contingent on your ability to jettison the toxic illusion of the ego self. And you must do this by passing through three sacred gates of enlightenment, each more sacred than the last. Ravi, kindly introduce them for us.

— Aye, boss, says the Indian dreamboat. The sacred gates of enlightenment are three in number. First is the glittering golden gate of non-allurement. Second, the intricate silver gate of non-comprehension. Third, the impenetrable iron gate of non-righteousness.

— He's not gonna know what any of this means, says Shel.

— Americans, Ravi grunts. All right, look, Tom. The only way to kill the ego illusion is by stripping away all the things you believe about yourself that aren't true. So, the first gate is targeting your outer beauty. To pass through, you have to accept the fact that you have none.

— Um—

— This'll be a breeze, says Shel. Can we all just agree right now that no one, anywhere, ever, would—*anywhere* I'm saying—would ever have sex with Tom?

— Do we have to agree to that, I ask.

— We do, says Crick.

— It's nothing personal, she adds. It's just I'd rather be with anyone else in this cave, and there's a ten-year-old child in here and a three-thousand-year-old Chinese woman.

— I think you're playing this up to help me through the gate, I smile knowingly.

— We're not, says Crick.

— Fine, whatever, I'm non-alluring. You can all go to hell.

— Well done, Initiate, cheers the Stonefish. Fastest I've ever seen that work.

NOT TO BRAG, but I'm told this first gate can be really tough sledding for most people, especially the young, beautiful people like Shelly who would seem at first glance to have a pretty strong counterargument insofar as most people everywhere are always trying to have sex with her.

To The Cause, though, we're all the same—a veil of particles and waves. And if you think about it, even the sexiest of waves is not particularly fuckable. With New Party donors, Shelly likes to talk about the "block universe," a conception of spacetime in which the past, the present, and the future all exist simultaneously.

But no one is very desirable in the block universe, because you're a zygote, and a toddler, and a corpse all at once. Which means you'd have to be a special kind of pedophilic, necrophilic, deviant bit of filth to find any of this remotely attractive. At least, I think that's what it means.

— **THE SECOND GATE**, resumes Ravi, is forged of intricate silver strands. To pass through it, you must accept that you know absolutely nothing about yourself or this world.

— Now come on, I protest. How can I seriously agree to that? I obviously know *some* things, like state capitals and such.

— States do not exist, says the Stonefish, let alone their capitals.

— Then how did I get a coffee mug that says it's better in Phoenix?

Crick rubs his temples in dismay.

— Fear not, Wilder, says the Stonefish. I believe these sad attempts at humor are the death throes of his insecurities. He's a tower ready to topple.

— Perhaps a little Socratic method then, says Crick. Tom, I want you to tell me something indisputable that you know about yourself.

— Okay. Well, I'm alive, for starters.

— That'll do nicely, he says. What does it mean for you to be alive?

— I don't know. I have thoughts. I have blood pumping in my veins.

— How do you do that trick, might I ask?

— How do I pump my blood?

— Right.

— Well, I—I mean I don't really know, I just do it.

— *You* do it?

— Of course.

— *You* pump the blood?

— Sure.

— But Tom, if you don't know how you're doing something, is it really *you* that's doing it?

— Of course, who else would it be?

Shelly smacks her forehead with her palm.

— Ugh, let me try something. Hi, Tom, she says.

— Hi.

— Is a rock alive, Tom?

— No.

— But a squirrel is alive.

— Yes.

— What about a virus?

— How big is the virus?

— Jesus lord, says Crick, we're getting nowhere. Tom, you're not alive because alive doesn't actually *mean* anything. It's just an arbitrary level of evolutionary complexity. And because we're narcissists, we decided that more complexity is better, even though most evidence points to the contrary.

— Tell him about the fly, says Ravi.

— Right, indeed. So the great Donald Hoffman proved that human sensory organs are an absolute dumpster fire, Tom. He used a concept called Evolutionary Game Theory and countless computer simulations to prove the more our sense organs evolve, the further away we get from objective reality. The more complex you become, the less veridical your perceptions. For truth seeking, you'd be better off as a fly.

— You're saying a stupid fly that can barely see, sees the world more accurately than I do?

— Right, because the clearer you see a fiction, the harder it is to break free. And the more elaborate the fiction gets, the further away you are from truth.

— So everything I *think* I know is based on faulty data collection?

— Garbage in, garbage out.

— And recognizing my own ignorance is the start of true knowledge?

— 95% of the matter and energy in the universe is dark, Tom. It's inaccessible to human senses. Best case scenario, we see less than 5% of reality. For you, it's probably less.

— Hmm, I say, turning this over in my head a few times. I suppose I can live with that.

Shelly and Ravi glance expectantly at the Stonefish. She takes a moment to consider, squinting her eyes in my direction.

— The second gate is passed, she decrees, and there's a collective sigh of relief.

— He's going through these at a remarkable pace, says Shelly.

— Let's not celebrate yet, Crick warns. We've now come to the last and most difficult gate of them all. You must accept, Tom, that you are not now, nor ever could be a good, righteous, or moral creature.

— We're all sinners—I get it. I was a non-snake-handling Catholic, I tell them.

— This is incorrect, says the Stonefish.

— Tom, it's not whether you're good or bad, Shelly explains. It's that good and bad don't mean anything without the passing of time. Good and bad are fungible—they're the same.

— I'm not sure I can get there, I confess to her.

— No, you cannot, says the Stonefish. Not without the sacred brew.

A FEW MINUTES LATER, with a blindfold over my eyes, Crick ladles a sour, viscous liquid into my mouth. As my head begins to swirl, I catch one last faint remark from Shelly— something about forgetting to strap on my diaper, which is never something you want to hear, but by the time it hits my brainstem I've already been reborn.

It's dark and cold outside, but I'm surrounded by love and warmth. My mother is holding me, and there are animals all around us—goats and sheep and oxen. She turns suddenly, noticing someone at the door to the barn. It's the three wise men. Only they're not men. They're long, spindly, ghost-like forms, translucent. I can hear them, but I don't understand. Their language is not sound. It all feels more real than real life, as if real life were only a dream. One of the forms approaches my mother, breathes into her, and she quakes, experiencing a violent vision. Her eyes roll back in her head, and light shoots from her sockets. It's a terrible sight, but I'm not afraid. I feel only peace and calmness and oneness with the ghosts and the animals. Now the form turns to me. It breathes into my mouth, and when breath touches breath, it condenses from vapor to mist. My whole body goes numb. My blood is lightening. I can see through time. All of human history in a blink.

I HADN'T NEEDED the diaper, thank God, but I spent the next half-hour vomiting my guts out, which was a promising sign according to the Stonefish. The more vomiting you do, the closer you've been to the elf machines.

As soon as I stop heaving, Crick and the others descend.

— What did they show you, Tom, he asks. What did you see?

— I saw a boy caught in a revolving door. He was being crushed, so I saved him. I was a hero. But then as time went by, the boy grew up to be a tyrant, worse than Genghis Khan. He slaughtered millions, and I was the villain who'd freed him. But then more time went by, and the nations of the world banded together to defeat the tyrant. It ushered in a golden age of cooperation and peace, and I was a hero again. But the peace left us vulnerable to an alien slug king and his brood of ravenous neonates. Also there was a Chinese farmer at one point.

— He's ready, says the Stonefish.

all your crying
don't do no good

THE YEAR WE ELECTED the robot president, everyone was getting high all the time.

This was after two terms of Desmond Thorp, the condo-building conman who took us, briefly, into a morass of American authoritarianism, but the AIs brought us back.

Thorp had tried to build a wall between North and South Dakota for some reason. He contracted the job to his son, and the whole thing turned out to be a money laundering scheme to fund disbanded Nicaraguan Contras who were launching a tech start-up in Ireland. So when that story broke, it cost him just enough votes—about five hundred on the margins in Wisconsin—to turn the election for Robert Otman, or President Microchip as he was known.

Otman wasn't the first robot politician, either.

The original politibot, dubbed Lincoln II, was a large language model trained on all of Honest Abe's old speeches, writings, and public statements. Unfortunately, nobody could understand a word it said. It was all four score this and ramparts that. Plus, they built Lincoln II as a fembot—you know, for equity reasons—and it's now widely felt that folks weren't quite ready for a female robot president.

But they got it right with Otman, yes sir.

He was trained on the sum total of all human knowledge, and they built him to resemble a genetic hash of all the former U.S. presidents. When he got into office, his first act was to bomb Canada, repeatedly, which didn't make much sense to us at the time. But then a couple years afterward, we learned those dirty Canucks had been plotting an invasion all along, and Otman's data-driven bombings had scared them off it, so score one for the machines.

Otman was so effective, in fact, he probably would have won a second term if it weren't for an unfortunate moment in the first Demopublican primary debate, when he had to be rebooted. His opponent, then Senator John D. Rockefeller Kennedy-Onassis Hemsworth the Third, Esquire stuck the dagger in and said: Folks, there won't be time for a reboot when he's sitting face to face with Putin Junior at the UN. Which is a weird line of attack, because of course there would be—the reboot only takes like eight seconds. But the line worked, Hemsworth won the race, and no one ever dared debate with him again until Shelly and I were in the soup.

WE HAD A LOT of free time back then, living in the caves, and some nights we watched the old debates. Shelly was a real savant.

— See, that's the kill shot, she tells me, pointing at the screen. When he sips that bottle of water, it's all over. Water's a crutch for the thirsty.

— Think you'd ever let Crick debate, I ask her.

— Oh God no, she says. He's like a sweatier, green Nixon.

Crick isn't paying attention. His eyes are glued to a chalkboard, where he's written out all twelve of the secret messages we've received from the machine elves.

— How does he get those again, I ask her.

— The messages? You know this. Dr. Grace talks to them.

— So Grace talks to the elves, and then he writes down what they said?

— Err—yeah, in a manner of speaking.

— Meaning what?

— Don't make a big deal of this.

— Shel?

— So after Grace talks to the machine elves, he smears his feces on the wall of the cave. Then Crick uses a neural network—

— Wait, what?

— Crick uses a neural network to analyze the vector patterns in the smear, and then we run it through an algorithm.

— You're kidding, right?

She shakes her head, ruefully.

— I never joke about The Cause.

— Hey, I've been meaning to ask you something, I tell her. When you first got here and took the initiation—the sacred brew. What was your vision like?

— Let's—not talk about that.

— Why not?

She takes a deep breath.

— It was about you and me, all right? Our future together.

— So, we *do* have a future.

— Yeah, sort of. Like I told you before, it's not the one you want.

The dull, constant pain in my heart is interrupted momentarily by a shriek from the lizard-skinned scientist behind us.

— It's an implant, he yells. A neurological interface—oh, those clever fucking elves!

Shelly looks nervous, probably because she's piecing together that this sequence of revelations ends with Crick performing brain surgery on the lot of us.

— This strange architecture, though, he mumbles to himself. It's recursive. It loops inward like a pretzel. I'd need a trillion dollars and the Corps of Engineers.

— Well you'll be president soon enough, says Shel.

— No, not soon enough, he growls back. The Stonefish has us chopping wood for the next five years. Did she tell you that? *Five more years of this shit!*

TRUTH BE TOLD, I was starting to get a little sick of all the wood chopping, myself.

I mean, we'd been living in the caves for eight months at this point, and aside from Crick's fecal pattern deciphering, we were mostly just taking drugs and chopping firewood. Sure, I'd seen the machine elves with my own eyes, and it was glorious. But how did I know for certain that any of it was *real?*

In fact, at the risk of becoming an unreliable narrator in your eyes, I should probably confess I'm not the world's best arbiter of reality these days—not since the ketamine therapy.

For years, psychiatrists had been dosing me with ketamine while trying to excavate the roots of my cognitive malaise—but the truth is, there was never much to find. My boyhood had been unremarkable. I was a middle-class kid in a two-parent home, in a decent neighborhood, with good schools.

Well, okay, I guess there was this one thing.

BACK WHEN I WAS seven and three quarters, what I wanted more than anything in life was a birthday party with the Ubermensch. And this was right after he stopped that big asteroid—do you remember? It was the height of his popularity. So I lobbied for weeks, and eventually I wore my parents down. They agreed he would make a brief appearance at my party, on the condition that I only view him from a distance.

I was thrilled. But things are never as good as you imagine them.

The real Ubermensch, of course, is a tall caucasian man— about six-foot-seven in boots. The actor my parents hired was maybe five-foot-six if we're being generous. He was also noticeably Filipino, had a wide assortment of neck tattoos, and was fully preoccupied—at the time I first caught sight of him—performing cunnilingus on my mother, on top of the dryer, in our laundry room.

My dad must have known this was happening, because the next thing I remember is the sound of his car's engine turning over, followed by a loud acceleration and the deafening crash of wood and plaster and drywall, as the north exterior of our house parted.

The short Filipino got caught between the back wall of the laundry room and two tons of American sport utility vehicle, and his torso essentially snapped in half, releasing a thick spray of blood and bloody entrails that coated my head, neck, and shoulders. *Use your regeneration powers, Ubermensch,* I shouted over his harrowing death rattle and my mother's tears. But it was no use. My hero lay in pieces, and my dad was surely headed for the electric chair. It was one of my three worst birthdays.

BUT WHAT IF that never actually happened?

If the machine elves were real — more real than real life — if my senses were hopelessly out of tune, if good and bad were fungible concepts, then what use were these memories, anyway?

The question began to gnaw at me.

I stopped eating.

I tried to cloister myself in a remote section of the cave system, but this very spot, in a tragic coincidence, was where Shelly and Ravi had been meeting secretly, every night since I'd arrived.

— Sorry you had to find out this way, she tells me.

— Yeah, rotten luck, Tom, says Ravi in between thrusts.

— It's okay, I tell them. We're all just circling the drain of oblivion. Who can even say what any of it means, or if any of it matters?

— Oh, I don't like the sound of that one bit, says Shelly. You'd better talk to the Stonefish. Nihilism will creep up on you, and our work here is much too important. You can finish anywhere.

— What?

— That last part wasn't for you.

— Sometimes I think enlightenment is a curse, I tell them as Shelly cleans herself off. I mean, historically, it's never worked out too well for folks like Socrates, Giordano Bruno—

— They shot Gandhi three times, point-blank, says Ravi.

— And meanwhile, all the ignorant people are out there living their best lives, while we're stuck in this cave, drinking brown cave water. Why even do this? What's the use of it?

Shelly's put her clothes back on, and she sits down next to me on the serrated rock I've chosen.

— Were you happy before all this, Tom? Were you living your best life?

— No, I probably wasn't.

— Course you weren't, she says. Because there's only one path for you, for any of us. And you can walk down it with your eyes closed if you want to. But you'll bump into a lot more shit that way, and when you get to the end, you'll have missed everything.

Only one path.

I didn't realize it at the time, but Shelly's words were a beacon, dripping into my awareness like Ravi's cum, which was running down her leg into my sock.

ONE NIGHT after nearly ten months inside the cave, when morale was at its lowest point, the Stonefish paid me a visit.

— What's really bothering you, Tom? What are you afraid of?

— Loneliness, I guess. Death?

— Well, I have some good news and bad news on that front. You can't die. You're eternal. You will always be here.

— What's the bad news?

— It's the same news, Tom.

She pulls off one of the animal skins around her waist and balls it up into a cushion for me to sit on.

— Why did I see myself as the baby Jesus, I ask her.

— We can only experience new things as rearranged pieces of what we've already known. As a former Christian, you instinctively reached for the Nativity. Shelly did something similar. I'm not surprised you're both trapped in the cycle—craving, pain, release. The whole ending to the Gospels fetishizes torture and suffering. They drill it into you when you're young. The first Howitzer House wasn't in the States, I think, it was on Calvary Hill.

— But how do I know any of this is *real*, I ask her. The visions, the machine elves. I've done psychedelics before. What if this is all just happening inside my own head?

— Well of course it is.

— Huh?

— How else do you see, Tom, but from inside your head? Your problem is you still think there's a difference between what's inside and outside. You're going to have to let that go, or you'll be miserable forever.

— Can you help me do it, I ask her.

— I think so, she says. You remember your Old Testament, don't you?

I nod, weakly.

— There's a part in Leviticus, she says, where it talks about making sacrifices in a certain way. You should go and find yourself a small bird. Something meek, and plain, and harmless. A turtledove. A sparrow. *And he shall cleave it with the wings thereof, but shall not divide it asunder.*

— I have no idea what that means.

— Our language is too rigid, she says. We don't have a good vocabulary for existential terms. But I had a clever student once, this was back in the 1940s. He was a writer like you are — Alan Watts, have you heard of him?

— I think so.

— He said when you write about existence, you have to lean into the contradictions. Take the words *to cleave*, which essentially mean their own opposite — to adhere and to split. And that's the paradox of knowledge, isn't it? To know a thing is to sever ourselves from it so we can see it from the outside. So the more we seek to know our own selves, the more we sever ourselves from the universe, and we become isolated and afraid, and we lash out in our fear and panic, and we war over senseless things, and we cling in desperation to illusions and shadows.

— I'm still not sure what it means, I tell her.

— Then just remember this. The body is one but has many members, she says. We are the meek little bird and the executioner, both. The knife and the sparrow. We are the microscopic cells in its anatomy, exploring the world as cells do, as beautiful fleeting bits of life, dancing into and out of existence like cosmic foam, forgetting and remembering and forgetting our connectedness to the whole. In and out. Again and again. Over and over. And you can know this, Tom. You can know it but divide it not asunder. For to find ourselves, we must always cleave the sparrow.

And that was the last thing she said before she died.

— **CAVE MEETING**, Crick calls out, and the rest of us assemble. We're going back to America. We've chopped enough wood. I know the Stonefish wanted five more years of wood chopping, but she's dead now.

— Are you insane, asks Shelly. Our all-seeing, infallible mentor's been gone for less than an hour, and you want to piss all over her last wishes?

— Her last wishes are unknowable, argues Crick. I for one choose to believe she spent her final minutes recanting everything she's been telling us—

— *You're wrong.*

The words burst out of me unexpectedly, in a strange, new, tenuous stream of consciousness.

— She wants us to follow The Path, I tell them.

— Whose path, asks Crick. *Yours?* That's rich!

— There's only one path, I say, reprising Shelly's mantra. All this wood chopping is symbolic, don't you see? She wants us to break down—to split, but not to sever. So we can find ourselves.

— You sound crazy, Shelly chides, but there's a glint of recognition in her eyes. How do you split something up without cutting it?

Crick smiles broadly—the winning smile of a born politician.

— Loop it inward, he says. Like a pretzel. Oh those clever
fucking elves!

contretemps

5

WHICH BRINGS US BACK to the start, more or less. After Crick's skull perforated on live TV, and Shelly turned his office into a presidential bootcamp.

We were fighting against the clock back then, with only seventy-two hours to fast-track my evolution from terrified staffer to plausible world leader.

It was a close shave, all right.

We practiced everything in that office: How to walk, how to smile, how to sidestep tough questions by circling back to an unrelated, indignant defense of Israel—you know, the basics. We even touched on ceremonial turkey pardons and workshopped some one-liners for the White House Correspondents' Dinner. By the eve of the election, I was a regular Mike Dukakis.

We were just about to close up shop for the night, when I noticed a small wooden box in the corner of the office—something I'd never seen before.

— It's got your name on it, Shel says, holding it up to the light.

For Tom—and only Tom. It's Crick's distinctive handwriting on a thin paper envelope, tied with ribbon around the box.

— Figures he'd try to control you from beyond the grave, she scoffs. And he doesn't even know your last name—how pathetic. Although, come to think of it—

— It's Small.

She makes a face: dyspeptic, then pitying.

— No one's gonna vote for a Tom Small, she says. Even I'd probably stay home. From now on, we're rebranding you as *Rik Vikington.*

— You're serious?

— As a Nordic rape fantasy. Let's get dinner.

I'm about to let go of Crick's mystery box when I catch a glimpse of four extra words, in a much smaller script, at the bottom of the envelope.

And not for Shelly.

— You go ahead, I tell her. I'm half-dead from all the turkey wrangling. Let's just meet tomorrow morning when the polls open.

She looks at me cross-eyed, but her hunger overpowers her suspicion.

— Suit yourself, Vikington, you rogue, she says and closes the office door behind her.

DEAR TOM, begins the letter, *do you remember what I told you? You're a true soldier. A true believer. And now it's time for you to make good on those qualities. Indeed, the fate of our whole universe depends on it. My hope is that watching my cranium burst open in the debate hall has convinced you I'm not fucking around here. But just in case you still aren't certain, I'll let you in on a secret. I poisoned the Stonefish.*

Huh?

It was necessary to do it, but immensely satisfying still. I've always hated her and those ridiculous gates of enlightenment. Do you really think a trained scientist would concede he knows nothing about this world? I know more than you could ever imagine. I'll give the Stonefish her due—she led me to Dr. Grace and the machine elves. But she's never understood the real dangers we face, and that primary danger is Shelly. Now I really can't stress this enough: Shelly must die.

What? No!

She's clever, and she's fearless, and her death is essential to my plan. She's a martyr who must never learn that she's a martyr. Do you understand me? You'll play along, won't you? She's just a stupid girl after all. A stupid girl who won't even offer you her stupid cunt.

You're a monster!

Look, you can blame me if it helps. But Shelly's time on Earth must end, and soon. That's the other danger we face — time itself. Now read this next part carefully. There are four holotapes inside this wooden box, and you must play them at precisely the right moments. The first tape — the green tape — is for your eyes only, after the inauguration, at midnight, and not a minute before. The rest of my instructions are on the tape. Do not, and I repeat, do not fuck this up please. Sincerely, Wilder Francis Crick.

I HAD TO SIT for a minute after reading the letter, and a cold, sinking feeling took root.

If I could lose the election somehow, I'd be free of Crick's snare. But it was wishful thinking. As soon as Crick shot himself, we went up forty points in the polls. Sixty points in Florida. I couldn't lose this election if I tried.

In fact, my coming victory was such a foregone conclusion, the President himself invited Shelly and me to the Oval Office on election night to watch the polls close, sip some bourbon, and plan together for an orderly transition.

Shelly could tell right away that something was wrong.

— We should talk about your Cabinet, she says on our ride to the White House. The New Party will have some input — Max Merchant will, I mean. That's the problem with taking his money. I'll be your Chief of Staff, obviously. I like Ravi for Secretary of the Device. What do you think?

— Are we really building that crazy thing, I ask her.

— What are you saying, Tom? That's the whole point of this.

— I know, I know. It's just that—well, what if Crick's not the man you think he is? What if there are things he hasn't told you?

Shelly gives me a look.

— Just listen, I tell her as our car pulls into the entrance. If it ever comes to it, I'll never let him hurt you. I'll keep you safe from him, no matter what.

— Are you high? Did you get any sleep last night?

— Please follow me, says the White House security chief, and we're shepherded along the colonnade on our route to the West Wing. President Hemsworth is standing outside the Oval Office with his hand extended.

— Consummate pleasure to meet you, Tom, he says with a genuine warmth that's disarming as shit. And my dear Shelly, you're a revelation.

He kisses her hand, and she blushes. This guy is really, really good at retail politics.

— Please come in, he says, beckoning us into the Oval. I'd like to introduce my wife, First Lady Kardashian.

She curtsies as well as one's able in a skin-tight, leather cocktail dress.

— Roller coaster of a campaign, says the President as we take our seats on the white couches. Thought I had it in the bag, to be honest. Stunning bit of stagecraft with the gun.

A porter hands Shelly a glass of bourbon, then one to me.

— Oh, but where are my manners, asks the President, turning to his wife. Here I am droning on, when Shelly's never had a proper tour of this place. Won't you show her the grounds, darling? You two can take the long way around. Take your time.

— I'd be delighted, says the First Lady, rising up from the couches and leading Shelly out of the room.

— Splendid, says the President as the door closes. You're completely fucked, Tom.

— I'm sorry, what?

— You're the most fucked little asshole who ever took a dick. I can't even look at you right now, you're so fucked.

He presses a button on the digital panel next to the couches.

— Come, he says into the microphone, and the door swings open.

The first entrant I recognize instantly: a large caucasian male, about six-foot-seven in boots.

— Greetings, citizen, says the Ubermensch.

I try to act unfazed, but my jaw is resting on the carpet. The other two figures I've never seen before, a woman and a man. The woman is bookish, mid-forties, in a lab coat. The man is older, late sixties, in military dress.

— This is Dr. Caitlyn Crowne, General H. Stewart Percy, and Jack Chalmers. They're about to tell you how fucked you are.

Caitlyn and the General nod politely while the Ubermensch pours himself a glass of water. One of the worst-kept secrets in Washington is that the Ubermensch is actually D.C. Chief of Police Jack Chalmers in a pair of thick-rimmed Warby Parkers. Literally everyone knows this, but it's just easier to pretend otherwise.

— The universe is dying, explains Caitlyn. We don't know why yet, but the physical properties of spacetime are breaking down.

— Holy shit, I say, coughing. So Crick was right all along?

— What exactly did he know, she probes.

— He said our universe is doomed, and that we're powerless to save it because we can't see objective reality. That's what his device is for—it's a neural implant. He named it the pretzel because its architecture loops inward. It isn't built yet. We got the blueprints from the machine elves.

— Is he drunk, asks the General?

— One bourbon, says the President. I don't think so.

— I too consume liquids to quench my human thirst response, says Chalmers, pretending to sip from his water glass.

— Err—

— Focus, Tom, says Caitlyn. How did Crick know the universe was dying?

— He thinks time is a block, I tell her. So everything we know that *will* happen—the end of stars, the black hole era, the heat death of the universe—it's all happening right now. We just can't *see* it happening because our human sense organs don't work for shit.

— This premise ignores the existence of the Ubermensch, says Chalmers. His physiology is much more advanced than yours—dozens more cone cell variations in his retina. And yet I can't see any black holes forming—I mean *he* can't—*hasn't*—seen any—he told me.

— Solid point, Chalmers, you weird fellow, says the President. Look, we can't just take someone's word on this, not unless there's evidence. Did Crick leave you anything, Tom? Anything we should know about?

The holotapes—I have to tell them about the holotapes!

But wait.

Crick warned me not to share them. He said the fate of our whole universe depends on my obedience and discretion.

Who do I trust more in this situation?

SHELLY TURNS TO ME as we're driving back to her hotel room on the waterfront, and she's the picture of classical elegance and grace.

— All right, buttfucker, she says. Now tell me why you've been shitting your pants all night.

— Can I come up to your room?

— Hon, we've talked about this—

— I'm not asking to—I just want to show you something. And we'll need a holoplayer.

She taps the rear-seat console, and a mini-player protrudes from the seat back. Good enough, I guess. I pull out Crick's holotapes and his deranged letter.

— From that weird box yesterday, she asks.

— You're the only one I trust with this.

I pop the green tape into the mini-player while she works her way through the letter, gasping at all the parts you'd expect.

Once she's done, I hit the start button on the console.

TOM, YOU IGNORANT FUCKING SCROTUM, yells the hologram. *I distinctly said to wait until after the inauguration! After, you walking embolism! Lucky for you, I foresaw this bit of reckless idiocy and took precautions. This tape is merely a decoy. The real first tape is the blue one—and don't you even think about* *playing it until after the inauguration, you ampullary polyp! Now straighten up and follow orders. And heaven help you if you've told Shelly about any of this!*

The message cuts off, and the mini-player deactivates.

— Put in the blue tape, she says. What are you waiting for?

— I don't—um—I'm just not sure that's such a great idea, Shel.

— Tom, stop being a pussy.

— It's not that.

— Tom?

— What is it?

— Stop.

— Shelly, come on.

— Being.

— I'm not doing it.

— A pussy.

— You can't bully me into this.

— Fine, what do we have then, three months to the inauguration? We'll just piss away all that time because you're a dickless virgin.

— I think time is a big part of this, I tell her. I just need you to trust me.

— Well that's never gonna happen.

— You've seen our future, right? You know what comes after.

— I don't want to talk about that.

— Then we're stuck in the cycle, Shel. Forever and ever. Craving, pain, release. Don't you want to break free of it? Because the only way out, I think, is to trust each other. To embrace each other as one. To follow The Path together with our eyes wide open and—

— Fine, she says. Fine, Tom—fine! Fuck you. I hate you. But I'll tell you what I saw.

everybody's
tripping
on roots

6

THE THEORY OF THE PATH—the single, inexorable path from which you cannot stray—is another paradox, like the black/white illusion. And that's a selling point, if you're inclined to believe my old mentor the Stonefish.

She said whenever you're humming along, making sense of the world, and then you're hit in the face with a gobsmacking, insurmountable contradiction like this, it means you're finally getting somewhere.

Now I'm no scientist or philosopher—obviously—but I learned a few things from Crick and the other cave dwellers in Heilongjiang, and one of the topics they used to fight about was *free will*.

Hard determinists will argue there's no such thing, that every action we take is the inevitable consequence of an infinitely complex causal chain, extending back to the birth of time itself. And if you had an all-powerful computer and the sum of all data in the universe, you could anticipate every action with absolute precision before it happened—Laplace's demon and all that.

But just when you think you've understood something in principle, quantum mechanics is often waiting in the wings to cock things up for you, and here's no exception. At the quantum level, we can prove there's a fundamental unpredictability and probabilistic nature to the behavior of particles. So hard determinism isn't possible.

And it certainly *feels* as if you have free will, doesn't it? That you have the power to decide one thing or another. Yet psychologists like Daniel Wegner insist this feeling of making a decision is a fraud—a delayed recognition of what your subconscious mind has already decided. And the brain, when pressed, turns out to be a remarkable bullshit artist.

Get a load of this.

In the 1960s, Roger Sperry severed the corpus callosum— the nerve fibers connecting our left and right brain hemispheres—in epilepsy patients, then studied the workings of those hemispheres in isolation. It was like Oscar Madison and Felix Unger. Each hemisphere had its own thoughts and motivations—its own *will*. This is all true by the way. And when Sperry asked the left hemisphere to explain why the right hemisphere was acting a certain way, and it couldn't possibly know the answer because their connection had been severed, do you know what happened next? The left hemisphere invented a bunch of crazy nonsense to explain it—just whatever random shit sounded plausible at the time.

Which suggests something ominous to me. That all our self-knowledge, all our dreams and motivations, our histories even, might be nothing more than a seat-of-our-pants, ex post facto rationalization of things that were decided billions of years ago by an ancient civilization of alien slugs.

So what's the remedy, Tom, you ask me. What should I do with this information? Well, some folks—your Obi-Wan Kenobi types—will say to let go of conscious thought altogether and act entirely on impulse. But if you've ever tried to live this way, you'll know it can't be done.

Because at every turn, you're going to find yourself with two distinct impulses, one per hemisphere. One tells you "stop," and the other says "go." And so you'll have to choose which one to follow, and this self-conscious act of interpreting your own divided mind is why you can't have nice things, because no matter how hard you try, or how desperately you desire it, no matter how much ketamine you take or heroin you inject, at the end of the day, for as long as you're here, there's just no getting away from yourself.

HERE'S A CASE IN POINT.

When she was fifteen, Shelly got sold into slavery. It happens more than you'd think, and not just around the Super Bowl.

She was in the foster care system in Illinois, without much supervision, and got recruited over social media. She took a bus to the Ozarks to meet a friend, met the friend, met the friend's buyers—a gang of Moscow-born human traffickers—and disappeared into the commercial sex trade. This was shortly after Putin fled Russia for "mysterious" reasons, and some of his ex-henchmen came stateside looking for work. Ivan Kuznetsov was their ringleader—a big Russian bear with a distinctly unpleasant smell, which is important, but you won't remember it.

I don't want to write about the next few years, and Shelly never gave too many details. I don't know what sort of toll it takes on a person, to be abused in that way for so long. I don't know if it builds slowly, or if you just hit a wall at some point, but Shelly says there came a time, eventually, when the two hemispheres in her brain reached a rare consensus and said: You really gotta kill these fuckers.

So she did.

She used a boxcutter, an iPhone power cord, gasoline, a bottle of cleaning liquid, and an acetylene torch. She took out four Russians in the process, stole a car, drove as fast and as far as she could without a license, and got arrested outside New Orleans.

They took her down to the station, and they asked her what happened. She still had blood on her hands and clothes.

— You wouldn't understand, she says. You haven't seen what I've seen.

— We've seen plenty, they tell her. And anyway, the power isn't in the things you see. It's in the way you process 'em—the story you tell.

— And I'm the author of the story, she asks.

— The one and only, ma'am.

— Hmm, she says. Let me see then. Okay, well, I guess what happened is this.

They lean closer.

— We were making a movie. Mom and Dad are stage magicians by trade, but they opened up a studio. Horror flicks and pornos, mostly. I was filling in for the prop master, and a couple of the squibs went off in my hand—you know those blood packs they use for gunshots? Freaked me out 'cuz I'm afraid of blood, and I just started running. I saw Mom's car in the lot and drove off, but I didn't have my phone or a GPS, so I got lost. There was a suitcase of old magic tricks in the trunk. I taught myself the Bengali Scarves routine—that's a killer routine. I did some shows on street corners, just panhandling, driving around, earning a few bucks for gas and hot meals, but never enough for a shower or a change of clothes. The car was hot and cramped, so I slept in alleyways. Used a dead raccoon for a pillow one time. That was six days ago. Thank God you found me, and I can get back to the studio.

— So nobody hurt you, they ask in disbelief.

— Nah.

— You're not in danger or nothing?

— No, sirs.

— But you said you've seen some things—

— I watched a dozen rats going ham in the crevice between two dumpsters—you ever seen *that*?

The officers give each other a look that says: We never slept on a raccoon, neither.

SOMETIMES I THINK enlightenment is a curse.

I told Shelly this once, in the caves, and I still say it's mostly true. People would rather believe a nicer version of events—a rat orgy, in this case, which is a real thing by the way.

So after a while, the two officers gave up and dropped the inquiry. And a few years later, Shelly took a tour of the Howitzer House in Deblaine, and then I met her in a sparsely furnished apartment near Somerset.

There's no love story for us, she told me. *You're always gonna want that, and it's never gonna happen. It doesn't matter what you do.*

And it made my blood boil to hear it, because I knew it was the truth right away. But what I didn't know back then— what I couldn't have known—is that she'd seen it in the sacred brew, from the machine elves themselves, just a few days after meeting Crick, who found her bunking with the rats in New Orleans.

He said: You're not going to believe this, but I'm the future President of America, and you're going to help me save the universe from extinction. And she said: Do you have a nice place to sleep and a change of clothes? And he said: No, we live in a cave at the moment, but it's temporary. And she said: Well is it at least a nice cave with an open floor plan? And he said: Not really. But she decided to go along, anyway.

AT HER INITIATION CEREMONY, Shelly didn't have as much trouble with the first gate as you might expect. Sex abuse victims often carry a low opinion of themselves, even when they look the way Shelly looks, which is to say *perfect*.

But the second gate was a slog. It took her nearly eight hours to break down and admit she was holding onto things that might not be true. Traumatic memories are often the hardest to abandon—the worst bits of ourselves, lodged in tight like wayward popcorn kernels, or a dozen rats going ham in the crevice between two dumpsters.

Now the third gate, as you know, cannot be breached without the sacred brew. So they strapped on a diaper, poured the thick, oily mixture in her beautiful mouth, and then she started to see things.

A hillside at first, with a gentle slope and a terraced field on either side. She's on the northwest shore of the Sea of

Galilee, surrounded by cypress and olive trees. She's about to give a sermon from atop the hill, and there's a crowd gathered below.

But when she looks down at the crowd more closely, it isn't made of people. It's a swarm of slender, fluttering little creatures, darting back and forth, aimlessly, mechanically. She tries to reach out her hand to them, but they aren't physically present. They exist in wispy intervals, like dissipating smoke, between the two points they're traversing. She cries out to them, and they respond the only way they can, by cracking open their heads and letting loose a projection of light—an invisible rope of fears and wishes. And when she crosses into that beam of light, her whole body goes numb, and she can see into the future.

I'M STANDING THERE with her, standing over a body. It's burned beyond recognition. The air is heavy and sour, suffused with ash.

— I did it for you, Shel, I yell to her through the smoke and the wind.

— What did you do?

— Stopped him—killed him. Then they burned the whole village down.

She stares back at the broken body below us, then down the slope of the hill to the smoldering remains of a desert encampment. Scattered bomb fragments, thousands dead.

— All for you, I say again, so that we can be together.

— But we never can, she says and tracks the anger rising in my chest, up through my neck and into my throat, recasting my voice as a villainous howl.

— I don't understand, I plead with her. What is so wrong with me? What disgusts you so much about me? I've done everything for you—

— It doesn't matter what you do, she says.

And then, as if to prove her wrong, I grab her, violently, and force her lips on mine. But it's like mist touching vapor. It's completely hollow. We're diaphanous like thread.

— Asshole, she says. I've tried to tell you, but you won't listen.

— Listen to what, I plead with her again.

We're inches from each other, but it feels like we're a hundred miles apart.

— It doesn't matter what you do, she says, because you haven't been born yet.

the monad
occupation

7

LOOK, WE'RE NONE of us perfect.

Sometimes you save the girl. Sometimes you kill a man, burn down his village, and force yourself on that girl. It all comes out in the wash, I'm told.

Besides, you can't be mad at a person who hasn't even been born yet, who hasn't even done the things you're mad about. That's like going back in time and killing baby Hitler. Would you have the stomach for that? Infanticide is in your wheelhouse, is it? Odd, don't you think, that everyone always talks about killing baby Hitler, but no one ever talks about going back to comfort him, help him through art school, and so forth. It's always kiss kiss bang bang with time travelers.

Speaking of which, I think it was Stephen Hawking who had an excellent proof against the existence of time travel. He said if time travel were ever to become possible at any point in our infinite future, we would know right now. Because all the tourist spots would be overrun with annoying fucking time travelers.

But what if those travelers didn't realize they were out of time?

How could you not realize it, Shelly argued: You're a thirty-six-year-old man, Tom. You've never had a girlfriend. Never kissed a girl. Never held someone's hand. Didn't that ever strike you as rather *odd*?

But here's the problem, I guess, with ketamine therapy or sacred brew. Once you're on the stuff, it's really hard to tell what's real. Or, to put it in terms my old mentor the Stonefish would use—if the ego self isn't real, then how real could its memories ever hope to be?

Strap in for this one.

You see a vision of the future, and in that vision you're surprised to learn you're a time traveler. But by seeing this vision, you're now aware of the fact. So you can't be surprised by it in the future.

But has anything really changed if the only difference is the mind of the observer in the vision? Is that mind even material? How would that realization move through space or time? To get at those answers, we'll need Crick's childhood hero, a man named Gottfried Wilhelm Leibniz.

Now Leibniz, by some accounts, was the first to document the existence of the machine elves. He called them *monads*—individual units of consciousness that constitute the very building blocks of reality. Monads are indivisible, said Leibniz, which means they must be immaterial, because anything that's physical you can split into smaller bits. And since you can't create material things from immaterial things, reality itself must be immaterial, and all the objects we perceive as physical creations like debate halls, and podiums, and apple-cheeked American children can't exist.

Donald Hoffman, back in our century, posits that spacetime is simply an interface—an abstraction manifested through human evolution that helps us interpret the reality of monads in ways our primitive brains can better understand. He compares spacetime to the desktop on your personal computer. Those little icons aren't real, of course. That's not the way computers *actually* work. There's no tiny recycling bin inside the monitor. But if I took away that interface, and now you had to toggle millions of transistors on and off, every time you wanted an eggplant emoji, you'd never get any emails done.

So here's the important part:

Materialists believe that everything about you, including thoughts and memories, are physical in nature. So they've been searching for reality and consciousness in physical phenomena like neurons and neural correlates.

Folks like Leibniz and Hoffman would turn materialism on its head. What if space and time, they ask, are manifestations of consciousness, and not the other way around?

It's a question that consumed Wilder Crick for most of his adult life. He spent nearly thirty years searching for the monads inside him. And when at long last he found the Stonefish and tasted her sacred brew, it was no ordinary vision he received.

He saw everything there is.

And then he saw that everything there is, is falling apart. Hopelessly breaking down, dissolving, in ruinous decay. Our own bodies, entire galaxies, the universe itself. Not some time soon, or in the distant future. But right now, always, before, and again.

It was a terrifying confirmation of everything he'd ever feared. And he emerged from this vision with a full diaper and a fulsome plan. We could save the whole world, he realized.

But we'd have to do it from the White House.

SPEAKING OF POLITICAL INTRIGUE, Shelly and I hadn't talked much between election night and the inauguration. I didn't know what to say to her, or even what it meant to be living "out of time."

Was I still the author of my own story?

I made a deal with myself, just in case. If at any point in the future it seemed I was inching toward murder, village arson, or sexual assault, I would take forty-eight hours to reconsider the merits.

And stories are often wrong, too.

After you're inaugurated, so the story goes, you get pulled into a small enclosure, torch-lit possibly, with weird Egyptian symbols on the walls, and there's a cluster of hooded figures who explain to you how Freemasons faked the moon landing and the Miracle on Ice, but it didn't happen like that.

I'd already learned the worst of things on election night: "The universe is dying, blah, blah, blah." If I'm being honest, I was much more concerned about Crick and Shelly than aliens or JFK—though, funny story, he was murdered by those pesky Canadians. And we already knew about extraterrestrials. The Ubermensch was living proof of it, even though his home planet Excelcion had exploded, and we hadn't found life on any others except for those goddamn space mites.

More importantly, I had a whole team now to worry about this stuff.

There was Ravi, my press secretary, whom I'd never really cared for. Something about his washboard abs, high cheekbones, and penchant for leaving seminal fluids inside the woman I love.

The New Party chose our VP, our Secretary of State, and some other key posts—all hand-selected by Max Merchant, of course. We retained a few folks from the previous administration: Dr. Caitlyn Crowne as our lead scientist, four-star General H. Stewart Percy as our national security advisor, and Jack Chalmers—the Ubermensch—as a special envoy. We even brought back former President Otman as a liaison for human/cyborg relations, but we mostly kept him in the attic.

And there was Shelly—my Chief of Staff—and of course the ghost of Wilder Crick, who was still pulling all the strings through a time-curated sequence of semi-abusive holotapes.

His next tape, the blue tape, was queued and ready to play in my bedroom, just as soon as the clock struck midnight. As it turns out, Crick had a pretty valid reason for the time delay. He must have known, somehow, that all hell was about to break loose that night.

I guess he'd seen it in the brew.

— **TOM, IT'S A CODE FUCKING RED**, says General Percy, barging into the West Wing dining room around 7pm.

— Huh?

— It means I need you in the Sit Room—now!

We dash across the access point, not even stopping to go through the magnetometers or the full-body scanners. No time for security. Things must be really, extraordinarily bad.

— How much do you know about the Janjaweed, he asks.

— The weed?

— The militia, says Shelly, entering the room behind us.

Shel, Ravi, and Chalmers take their seats around the conference table, and we all gaze skyward at a floating projection of the Earth.

— This is Africa, Tom, says Percy. Do you know about Africa?

— I'm not brainless, I fire back.

— Can't make any assumptions—there's no fucking time. Now Tom, over here is Sudan. That's Khartoum, the capital. The Blue Nile and the White Nile—

— Wait, there's more than one Nile?

— Not the time, bud, says Shelly gently.

— Okay, but that's a genuinely surprising fact—

— They're actually tributaries, explains Ravi.

— Ah, I see.

— Would everyone shut the fuck up please, says the General. Jesus Christ almighty. Now Tom, there have been dozens of military coups in Sudan—dozens! That's a distressing number of coups, if you're wondering.

The floating holographic projection morphs into a dark-skinned, balding man with square glasses.

— Omar Al-Bashir, continues Percy. The former head of state. He's besieged. He needs to fend off coup plotters in the west, but his soldiers are pre-engaged in a coup defense down south. He needs more men. So he calls up the worst people on the planet—a Moscow-backed paramilitary called the Janjaweed.

— What makes them so terrible, I ask.

— Oh, this and that, says Percy. How do you feel about the widespread, systematic, and genocidal raping of children?

— I'll just hold my other questions.

— Would you? Now after the fighting ends, al-Bashir gets sent away and tried for war crimes. But the Janjaweed's still hanging around, right? That's the problem with empowering a paramilitary. They never actually leave. And now their top man is a real-life psychopath named Abu Rahim Khalil.

— Al-Saghir, says Ravi.

— Right, they call him *al-Saghir*, which means "the little one."

— But he's not little, says Ravi. He's strong and mighty and glorious.

— Yeah, whatever, calm down, says Percy. Like I was saying, al-Saghir is a genuine nutcase—a zealot. He goes to war against the government of Sudan. Even worse, he says he's done taking orders from "Russian dogs." And you can guess how that goes over with Putin.

— Not well?

The General nods, gravely.

— This is all classified now, he says. Putin sends ten long-range nuclear warheads to the Sudanese government. It's all for show. Deterrence. He knows they aren't crazy enough to use them. He just wants al-Saghir to sweat a little. Bring him to heel. But then something truly unexpected happens.

— What? What happens?

Percy's eyes fall on Chalmers, who's been conspicuously nursing a Pepsi this whole time.

— An alien spaceship crash-lands in Southern Egypt, he resumes, which is only a few hundred miles from Darfur. And the force of the impact and the radiation signature on the craft looks a helluva lot like a nuclear strike. So Putin just assumes it was one of the Soviet nukes.

— Holy Chernobyl, says Shel.

— And now Putin thinks he's well and truly fucked, right? Because they'll trace the warheads back to Moscow.

— So *that's* why he fled Russia.

The General nods.

— By the time he realizes the error, it's too late—all his loyalists are gone. So Putin's bastard son takes the reins, negotiates the Kiev Accords with Tom's predecessor, and with the Ubermensch around to keep both parties honest and those sneaky Canadians in check, we had nearly eight years without an existential crisis.

— Why are you saying that in the past tense, I ask the General.

He winces as the holographic projection morphs into a ghastly fireball and mushroom cloud.

— Tom, we just received these images an hour ago. A nuclear test detonation, way out in the desert. Al-Saghir's men must have stumbled on the loose nukes in Khartoum.

— Fuck me sideways, says Shelly. So now the Janjaweed has nuclear weapons?

Ravi cocks the Kalashnikov rifle he's been hiding in his lap.

— As a matter of fact, he says, we've had them for years.

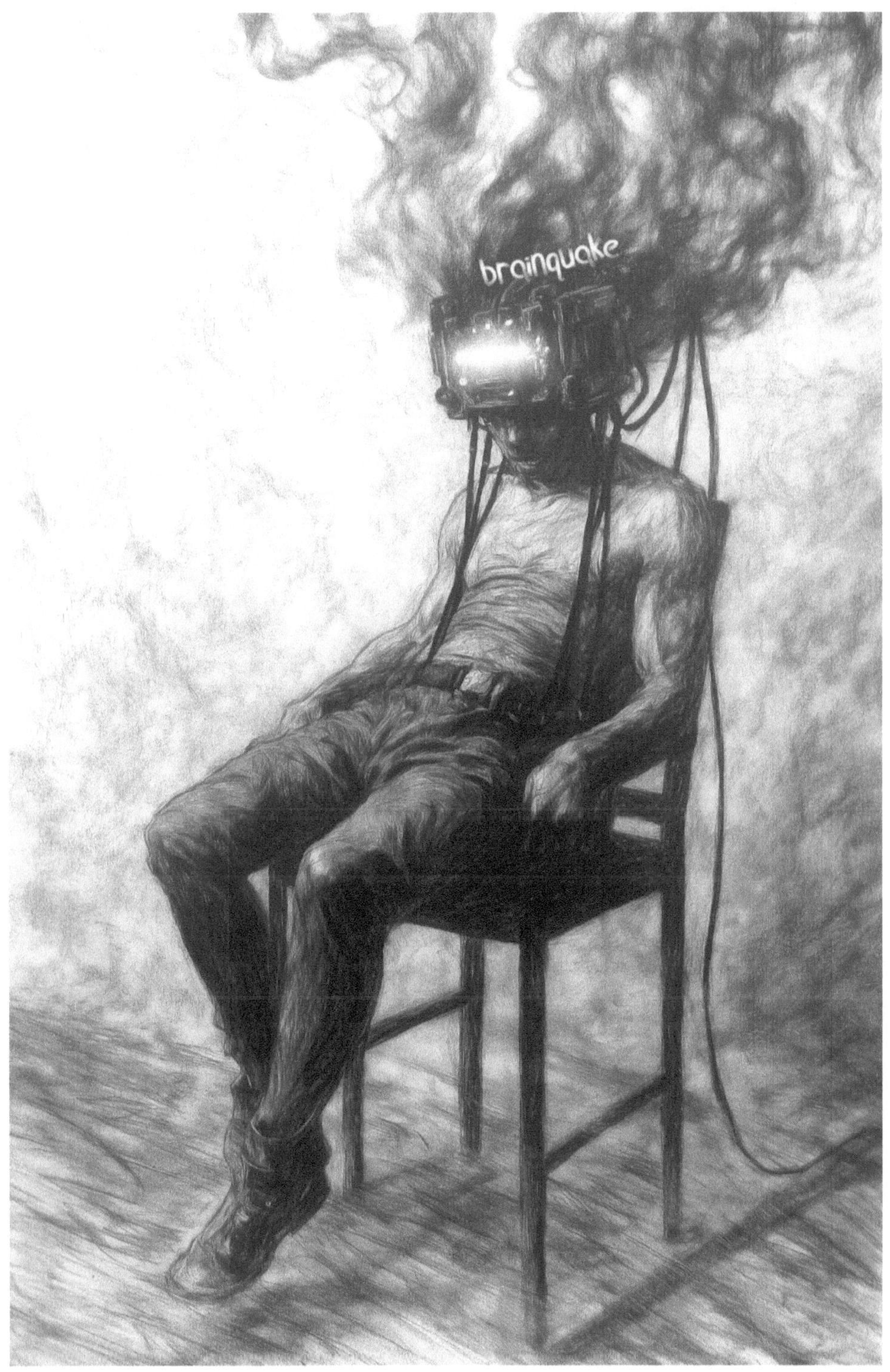
brainquake

8

CULTS, I'VE COME TO REALIZE, are precariously dependent on their leadership. There's no succession plan with cults. You stop the leader of the cult, that's it. Because the whole thing's a show, running mainly on the strength of its charismatic star.

Desmond Thorp is a prime example—the only American president with a billion-dollar brand, reality TV residuals, and a fraudulent dental school.

There's a sad ending to it, though.

After he lost that squeaker election to Otman in '28, he tried to overthrow the government, as one does, by dispatching a mob of violent protesters to the U.S. Capitol. But he picked a bad day for it. A gentle rain deterred all but his most ardent supporters, and the ones who came were distracted by a free screening of *Top Gun: Maverick*, which

Otman had presciently organized in the Capitol's visitor center. So score one more for the machines.

Crick, too, was a fine cult leader, even after his head exploded.

But Ravi—a cult leader? No, I don't think so. Certainly not a leader of the fiercest monad cult there's ever been.

Al-mu'aqqibat.

Oh, you thought Crick's obsession with the monads was sui generis? No. There had always been others, most notably an intrepid band of monad seekers in Southern Egypt, named for a special class of guardian angels in the Quaran—the ones who follow after.

Al-mu'aqqibat.

Led by a living shadow, the Hidden Imam, the returning *Muhammad al-Mahdi*, a descendent of the Prophet whom Islamic eschatologists foretold would lead the Muslim faithful to a new world order at the end of time.

And when it comes to cult leaders, you should know this: The Mahdi is undefeated.

AS FOR RAVI, he contained multitudes.

Was he a cunning double agent? Without a doubt. A passable press secretary? No argument here. A skilled tantric sex practitioner? If you insist, but I wish you wouldn't.

For one thing, his name wasn't actually Ravi, but rather Usama Quereshi, which I think I mentioned at the jump, but you probably brushed past it.

He'd been working in underworld security after a dishonorable discharge from the Indian military over a tantric sex dispute, which is the leading cause of officer decommissioning in that part of the world.

Angry and resentful at his former superiors, Usama took an ill-advised job smuggling dimethyltryptamine through the Jaisalmer Military Station in Rajasthan, which was immediately hijacked by Al-mu'aqqibat commandos. So, finding himself outgunned and unwilling to die for someone else's DMT, Usama cut the best deal he could and joined the Mahdi in Egypt.

But he was very much a work in progress.

All muscle, no guts, the Mahdi said of him. Not nearly fervid or deranged enough to help end civilization. So they sent him off to train with the Janjaweed in Sudan—the worst people on earth—while the Mahdi crafted plans for infiltrating Crick's inner circle and stealing his monad-seeking brain device.

Months later, Usama returned to Egypt with a stunning bit of news:

Al-Saghir was in possession of ten long-range nuclear warheads, which he'd been hiding, very quietly, for nearly a decade. Waiting for the end of time. Waiting for the Mahdi to return.

So the plan went into motion. Usama became Ravi. He sought out Crick and the Stonefish in the caves of Heilongjiang, and he gained their trust by serving as Crick's bodyguard—which is a key role to fill when your green-tinted boss is breathtakingly unpleasant and likes to pick frequent, unnecessary fights with the Teamsters Union.

Ravi fooled us all so thoroughly, Shelly brought him into the White House with a top-level security clearance. She also brought him up to her cervix, but we won't talk about that.

— **RAVI, WHAT THE HELL**, Shelly barks in surprise.

— *Allahu Akbar fawqa kaydi l-mu'tadi!*

— I thought you were Hindu, I gasp in his direction.

— Everyone assumes that, but there's two hundred million Muslims in India, you dicks.

— What do you want from us?

— You know exactly what I want, he says. Your precious monads.

Shelly's eyes bore into mine, imploring a heroic plan of action, but my brain's still numb from the history lesson. There's no Secret Service in the Situation Room. No weapons or defenses. Abrupt, amidst the silence, I can hear the faint sounds of clicking metal, the nervous unbuckling of a leather belt.

— I said *monads*, yells Ravi. And honestly, General, take a breath, will you?

He raises the gun.

— Okay, wait, I cry out. You're forgetting something, Ravi—Usama, whoever you are. You hadn't counted on the Ubermensch! He could grab that gun from you before your finger hits the trigger.

— He could, indeed, if he were here, says Chalmers.

— No, but—what?

— Oh for fuck's sake, says Shelly.

— Just take the gun! You're impervious to bullets!

— What on earth are you implying, coos a doe-eyed Chalmers.

— Unbelievable—

Ravi re-cocks the rifle.

— I'm going to enjoy this, he says. Even more than when I poisoned the Stonefish.

— I thought Crick poisoned the Stonefish, whispers Shelly.

— Did he really? That's remarkable we'd pick the same day for it.

THUNK!

Ravi shoots the General in the chest, then Chalmers, who pretends to die in an elaborate improvisation.

— All those secret messages, says Ravi. Those blueprints. I tried to steal them from Crick and couldn't parse a word of it. But *you*, Tom, his successor. He must have told you how to build it.

— I swear he didn't! Unless it's on one of those holo—

— Shut the fuck up, Tom, says Shelly before I can finish the thought.

— It's good advice, Ravi chirps. Neither one of you has to say another word. I'll just pull what I need from Tom's mind.

He reaches down into the satchel by his feet and retrieves one of Shelly's old focus group machines—the kind that traces your biological feedback and runs it through an algorithm to determine whether or not you're in favor of our retconning Hitler's genitals.

— He'll brainquake, Shelly yells as Ravi straps the headset to my skull.

He turns the dial to the right, all the way.

— Full power, you heathens!

— Please don't, Shelly begs of him, and she seems genuinely concerned for my welfare in this moment.

Wait, is this what love is? Fondness at least? My brain and heart are both confused and ready to burst. The pain is too intense—far worse than ordinary spleen combustion.

I fall to the ground, grasping for the dial in Ravi's hand.

There's no one else in sight. Only Chalmers, who's splayed out on the carpet beside me, furtively glancing at his watch.

WHEN I SNAP BACK TO LIFE, I'm alone.

Ravi, Shelly, and Chalmers are gone, and the General is still dead.

From the hallway, I can tell the whole White House is deserted. Something terrible has happened.

The alarm on my phone begins to chime—it's midnight.

Of course it is.

I make a beeline for the Residence, where Crick's blue holotape is queued and ready to play.

Here comes the other shoe.

LOVELY TO SEE YOU, TOM, says the smiling hologram, and I'm put instantly off-balance by the lack of angry personal epithets.

Sorry I had to take such a harsh tone before, but I wanted your full cooperation. You see the method to my madness now—why I needed your brain pristine? I'm really not the monster you think I am. I know I look like one, and I can be a bit intemperate at times. But everything I've done, I've done for you, my beautiful son.

Huh?

Well, some of it was for me, and for the universe, but you're a non-trivial beneficiary. Now I'm going to tell you some things, my precious child, that you might find troubling to hear—or rather one thing in particular. Shelly is your biological mother. That's right, we fucked. You were right to be suspicious.

Goddammit!

If it's any consolation, I hardly enjoyed myself. I was thinking of an immersion blender the whole time. But we did the deed so we could get your help to solve this whole universe dying problem, and I have to assume it's gone well enough, because if you're listening to this, the universe is still around.

To be honest, I'd watched enough time travel movies to suspect that Shelly and I might be related. But I was hoping for ancestral cousin, or great-grandmother at worst, which I know is still bad, but it's not Oedipus-bad.

One thing you might be wondering, Tom, is why I've kept you in the dark, or why I sometimes get things wrong. The answer to both is quantum mechanics—it's always waiting in the wings to cock things up for you. A fundamental unpredictability in the behavior of particles that even the machine elves can't surmount. But there's a way to put a lid on it. You just have to stay blindfolded. Limit the variables. Remember how we talked about human vision and fly vision, and how the shitty fly vision is actually more veridical? Same principle here. Complexity is the enemy. Observation breeds complexity, and complexity breeds uncertainty. The more you look, the more times you open the box, the more opportunities for Schrödinger's cat to jump out and bite you in the dick. Do you understand? It's why Shelly can never learn that she's a martyr. And it's why you must never, ever show her my letter or these tapes.

Err, so—

I repeat, if Shelly were to realize her role in this, it would create a cascade of uncertainties that I simply cannot navigate. The universe will not survive. But I'm sure I needn't worry about it—you've got things under control. Now let's talk about the pretzel.

Err, about that last part, though—

I've hidden step-by-step building instructions in a secure enclave within former President Otman's CPU. He'll know how to access it. And there's something else in there, too—a gift for you.

A gift?

Tom, your mission is to manufacture my device by any means necessary and implant it into Dr. Grace's enormous head. Do not test the device on yourself or anyone else. Do not let this technology fall into the hands of Al-mu'aqqibat or anyone else. Do not attempt immigration reform as president—it's not worth the political capital. And above all else, protect these holotapes! The red tape, Tom, is your one-shot, last-gasp, emergency escape hatch. But you must only use it if things look absolutely hopeless. There is a terrible,

The holoplayer deactivates, and I'm left alone with my despair.

Shelly and Crick, my parents? I look around for some brooch pins to gouge my eyes out, but there's only a tall, presidential-looking android in the corner of the room.

— Otman?

— Hello, Tom.

— How are you still here? The whole building was cleared—

— They never found me. I spend most evenings in a storage crate.

— I'm so confused, I tell him, blubbering. I think I've doomed mankind. Shelly knows way too much. I didn't listen. My head is spinning. Where is she—is she all right? What have I done? There's a lump in my throat. I feel feverish—

— There, there, says the politibot. I have a gift for you.

— From Crick?

— Indeed, says Otman, inserting a portable drive into his ear port. Two of your original memories—the greatest hits.

— My *original* memories? What does that mean?

— Calm yourself and focus, Tom. No one is doomed here. Not yet, at least.

— But what the hell are you telling me? Are you saying my own memories aren't true?

Otman docks the flash drive in a small laptop computer.

— Nothing ever is, he says, until we make it so.

i am a
strange
loop

IT CAN BE TORTUOUS, I know, this tour of everything I've seen and learned. It can be plodding and pedantic, I'm aware.

But if I'm ever going to help you with your problem — you know, the reason you're confused and unhappy, the reason you wake up in the night with a pit in your chest — if you want me to solve this for you, there's a decent bit of background you're still missing.

I'll make it as painless as I can, of course. But no one learns philosophy for fun. Or if they did, they'd be admitting to the world, and to themselves, that their mental construct of enjoyment, their Platonic ideal, has been badly mismanaged.

So let's fight through it, shall we?

THUNK!

A tree falls in Dublin, but Irish philosopher George Berkeley can't hear it. He's all the way out in Waterford.

A few days later, he gets a letter from Callum, one of his chums at Trinity College. *It finally happened, Georgie,* says the letter. *That big sucker near the bell tower. I really wish we could have been there to hear it come down—a crash for the ages, and I know how you love a good felling.*

He does, but not like this.

False alarm, George writes back to Callum. *That crash never happened, because we weren't around to hear it.*

Put another way, when folks like Donald Hoffman assert that human sense organs are a dumpster fire, and we can't possibly perceive objective reality with such pitiful equipment, they're also making a second, implicit assertion:

Objective reality exists.

What you perceive as a tomato might not be a tomato, says Hoffman. It might not be red, or round, or even three-dimensional, but it's based on *something*. There must be *something* out there for our strange human minds to misinterpret.

But why should we assume this?

What if, as idealists like Berkeley believed, all reality is subjective and contingent on the observer?

And I raise this question now because an idealist's take on reality—which goes way beyond even the zaniest ideas of Leibniz and his monads—seems to be, largely, what quantum mechanics is trying to tell us.

QUANTUM BAYESIANISM, or QBism for short, is a modern interpretation of quantum theory that suggests we can influence the probabilities of quantum phenomena with our own personal beliefs and perceptions.

That's a pretty radical idea, which requires our leaving behind some of the security blankets we've all grown rather attached to, like the notion of objective truth, or a "God's-eye-view" of the universe. It's a view we may never get to see for ourselves—we're not gods, after all—but it's still a comfort to believe it's there.

So when quantum physics introduced us to the concept of *superposition*—meaning particles can have multiple values simultaneously—we twisted ourselves into knots looking for ways to reconcile this new feature with our stubborn belief in objective reality.

That's how we arrived at "bizarre" theories like infinite parallel worlds, splintering away from each other every time someone makes a quantum observation. Possible, I guess, and great for the Marvel franchises, but is it really necessary? Aren't we trying a little too hard to bend reality to our will?

Alan Watts, one of the Stonefish's favorite disciples, drew this helpful distinction in 1951:

Belief clings, he wrote. Faith lets go.

THE FOLLOWING IS PRESENTED *by Seagan's Anti-Rust Coating. The underbody protection you can trust—against rust.*

— Otman, did Crick sell commercial time in my memories?

— We had a funding crunch a few years back, and we did what we did.

There's something strange about watching your own memories play on a laptop screen. The production values are terrible, for one thing. There's no soundtrack. The shot compositions feel random at best.

I'm barely ten years old from the looks of it, which means this happened over a quarter century ago, but it's clearly a vision of the future.

— Strip down, Tommy, says a middle-aged woman. It's time for your radiation meds.

I'm sitting in a windowless capsule, scribbling in a workbook. The woman is my chief science advisor, Dr. Caitlyn Crowne.

— Has it been twenty minutes already?

— Don't fuss, dear, she says. You know we need to get this fluid directly into your spinal cord, sixty times each day.

— Yeah, yeah.

Caitlyn brandishes a small harpoon and jabs it into my back. I scream in anguish, then vomit quietly into a paint bucket.

— See, that wasn't so bad.

There's a knock at the door.

— Calvin, is that you, she asks through the barrier.

— The one and only, he replies.

— Can I get you an oxygen suppository, Cal?

— Just had one, thank you.

I'm preoccupied with the homework problems in my workbook, it appears. The math is unrecognizable.

— What brings you around, Cal?

— Same as always, he says. You're quite sure you won't sell me the boy? He'll fetch ten-thousand credits in the cobalt mines.

— Twice that, she says. But Shelly asked me to look after him. And she sacrificed so much for us.

— A real hero, it's true—damned amazing what she did, taking down the Madhi like that. I mean, things aren't great these days with all the black holes and Hawking radiation, but at least we're not all speaking Arabic.

— Can I get you an oxygen suppository now?

— Yes, it's almost time—

— Okay, stop this for a minute, I tell Otman.

He hits the pause button on the laptop screen.

— Is it just me, or is this future rather horrible?

— It's not ideal, he concedes. But as an android, I'll be immune to the biological effects.

— And we could stop it—prevent this from happening by building the pretzel?

— Crick thought so. I have my doubts.

— Why's that, I ask him.

— Tom, have you ever known anything to get better through human intervention?

— Err, well—

— Let's just finish the memory, says Otman.

In a true act of mercy, he fast-forwards through the bulk of the suppository insertion. On the screen now, Calvin glances down at my homework book.

— Ah, Slug Theory, he says.

— This unit doesn't make much sense, I tell him.

— None of it does. But it's still better than that pesky "science" we used to have. Can you believe what they tried to sell us on consciousness? The mere collapsing of quantum wave functions in the microtubules of neurons? I'll take the alien slugs seven days a week and twice on Sundays, thank you very much. At least those slugs have some respect for the sanctity of life.

— What was it like in the old days, I ask him.

— She never told you?

— We don't talk about it, says Caitlyn. Crick's orders.

— Ah, yes, says Cal. That scaly old bastard—does he even come around to visit? Too busy hopping starships with Max Merchant, I'll bet. Heard they're living up there on the comets, mining excelcium dust.

— It's time for The Screeching, says Caitlyn. Everyone put in your plugs.

Cal, Caitlyn, and I grab heavy-duty ear protectors from under the couch, just as an excruciating, high-pitched sound envelops the capsule. Even with the muffling of the ear plugs, it's the loudest, most unpleasant noise I've ever heard—like peacocks screaming into a megaphone. It plays continuously for forty minutes (or two radiation shots and a half-dozen oxygen suppositories, if you're keeping track). Thankfully, Otman holds his finger on the fast-forward button.

— I'll never get used to that, says Cal, removing his ear plugs. But it's worth it, I guess, if it keeps those colossal, irradiated mosquitos off the energy towers. Anyway, I'm off to buy another case of Seagan's Anti-Rust Coating before they regroup. If there's a better way to protect your car's underbody from rust, I haven't found it—and only fifteen credits when you use promo code: memories.

The movie cuts off abruptly.

— One down, one to go, says Otman. How are you feeling so far, Tom?

— All right, I guess. Can't say I'm looking forward to The Screechings.

— You mean looking backward.

— What?

— Never mind. We could rest a little before the next memory, if you want.

— No, let's get it over with.

The second movie begins, and I look like me—the current me. So this must be a fairly recent memory. I'm in a small, silver chamber. Everything is shiny and sterile, like a hospital or a morgue. There's a knock at the door.

— He's ready for you now, says a familiar voice I can't quite place.

The doors open behind me, revealing a much larger chamber with similar decor. A frail, green-tinted patient lies atop a mobile hospital bed, connected to all manner of whirring medical machines. To his left is a tall figure I've only seen before in pictures, when he was much younger— Maxwell Merchant, the world's first trillionaire, space magnate, and purveyor of juvenile Internet memes that are only antisemitic in an ironic way.

To Crick's right is the owner of the voice I couldn't place. He has the same black teeth and massive forehead, but he's not the feral sadist I remember. Whereas young Dr. Grace ran hot, there's a preternatural coolness that surrounds his older self—as if he's seen things the rest of us simply haven't, or couldn't.

He's been pretzeled, is my working theory.

— It's good to get reacquainted, Tom, says the older, wiser Grace.

— Have we met before?

— In a way, he says. Technically, it hasn't happened yet, but I remember it well. The last time I saw you, we were in China, and I'd just poisoned the Stonefish.

— Who's the Stonefish, and why did you poison her?

— Well, I was poisoning everyone back then. I was a real hellraiser.

— Come closer, my son, Crick calls out, weakly, from his deathbed.

He looks a hundred years old in this memory, and his health is clearly failing.

— How are you getting on, Tom, he asks. I don't think I've seen you since our move out here to the comets. Hell of a place Merchant built, don't you think? And not a second too soon with the Earth getting all—well, you know—what's the word I'm looking for?

— Swallowed, says Grace.

— I've been making the best of things, I tell Crick. It's been difficult, though. Those space mites keep getting more resourceful. You remember my uncle Calvin?

— Vaguely.

— They chewed off a part of his face to distract us while the queen laid eggs in his penis. When it finally burst last week, it took out the whole north section of the habitat.

— Ah, yes. Terrible thing, that. But look, I've summoned you here for a very important reason. I'm going to need you to travel back in time.

— Is that possible, the younger me asks with astonishment.

— Not only is it possible, Tom, it's the whole reason you were born. Your mother and I had exactly one motivation for creating you, and it's this. Everything else you've done for the last thirty-five years has been entirely meaningless. If someone ever tried to watch the movie of your life, they'd only need about ten minutes of childhood for atmosphere, and then this moment right now. The rest would be completely extraneous.

— Well *that's* depressing, says the older me to Otman.

— Hard to argue with the time we're saving, he replies.

Back inside the movie, Crick strains to lift himself up, just slightly, so he can get a better view of me.

— Tom, we're going to rescue the universe—the four of us. You, me, Grace, and Merchant. I've been preparing for this for fifty years, and I've tried to hold out as long as I can, to get everything in place for you, but I'll be dead soon. We all will, one way or another. Killed instantly by a black hole, vaporized by cosmic rays, or dying slowly from a staph infection after your penis explodes with space mites. It doesn't really matter how it happens—

— Err, I feel like that last one—

— You're missing the point, Tom. It's all for nothing unless I send you back, says Crick.

— How does it work—this time travel?

Dr. Grace now sidles up with a syringe of blue liquid.

— Are you familiar with the quantum-based Orch OR theory, Tom?

— Not really. I majored in Slug Sports Medicine.

— Imagine that consciousness is merely the result of quantum activities in the mind, and those activities produce a continuum of experiential states—from connected consciousness to disconnected dream states, to complete oblivion, and everything in between. One of those modulated states is a bit like astral projection—you won't be able to touch anyone, but they'll be able to see you and talk to you.

— Could they put something on me, like a headset?

— Well, that's sort of a gray area. Point is, Tom, you're not actually traveling anywhere. You're just accessing a different part of your mind.

— Will it hurt?

— No one's ever tried it before. In fact, we've only just mined enough excelcium dust to cook up the induction serum. Grace tested it on a few space mites, and they all died instantly. So, look, if this doesn't work out for you, we can always give it to the exterminators.

Dr. Grace raises the syringe to the base of my neck.

— Um, don't you need my consent for this?

— There aren't any lawyers left, Tom, and I'll be dead in a few minutes. Just remember your mission.

— But you haven't told me what it is—

— Haven't I? Fuck, I think you're right. Cleave the sparrow, Tom.

— What?

— The sparrow. Cleave it, man.

— I don't—*what*?

Grace jabs the syringe into my younger self, and I swear I feel it burning in my older self, too.

As the movie shuts off, Otman stares at me in astonishment.

— You're—you're a *projection*?

He tries to place one of his metal hands on my face, but it's just as in Shelly's vision. There's an unbreachable separation of space, time, and body.

— I don't believe it, he says, marveling at the strange sensation. But at least you won't feel the blast.

— Feel the what?

— I've been waiting for a good time to tell you this, he says and glances downward at my glowing, blue torso.

There's a cord around my waist.

It's holding up a complex arrangement of fuel rods, oxidizers, and digital circuitry, and it dawns on me—a little slowly, I'll admit—that they've emptied out the White House because I'm wearing a nuclear bomb.

the bow and
the lyre

10

THE REPUBLICANS WERE ADRIFT.

As I've argued before, cults can rarely survive without their leaders, and Thorp was facing a litany of prosecutions for, among other things, stealing confidential nuclear schematics and using them to wallpaper a Pentagon-themed steak house in Palm Beach.

In 2032, Thorp campaigned for the Republican nomination from a Leavenworth prison cell, and he would have won another term—handily, given the price of eggs—if not for a catastrophic lack of campaign funds.

You see, Thorp's small donors were all tapped out, and the corporate bundlers were sick of funding his legal defenses. Increasingly, the GOP was beholden to a single megadonor—the world's first trillionaire, electric car maven, and racehorse-grade ketamine evangelist, Maxwell Merchant.

And Merchant had a lot of ideas.

One of them was to build an island out of floating shipping containers in international waters, so he could openly flout federal statutes. Another was to harness the destructive power of synthetic tornados.

You might assume these strange gambits would appeal to a man like Thorp, but you'd be wrong. His platform had become increasingly single-minded in its focus on crushing Joy Behar. And using tornados for the job just seemed ostentatious.

Also, Merchant was a *transhumanist*, which means he believed strongly in the convergence of human biology and advanced cybernetics.

Put it all together, and Max was much more inclined in '32 to back a robot incumbent like Otman than to help resuscitate a Grand Old Party now headquartered in a supermax federal prison.

So Merchant pulled his funding.

The Republicans went kaput.

And the Democrats, being Democrats, invited their former adversaries into a new, egalitarian conglomerate called the *Demopublican Majority Party*.

As their unity candidate, they chose the most popular man in America, a bafflingly charismatic senator named John D. Rockefeller Kennedy-Onassis Hemsworth the Third, Esquire, who defeated Otman in the first-ever Demopublican primary, won the presidency unopposed, made peace with

Putin Junior, and birthed an epoch of harmony and forbearance that made hardliners like Merchant absolutely furious.

He tried to wait it out.

It's only four years, he told himself, eight at the most. But when Congress repealed the 22nd Amendment so Hemsworth could run for additional terms, Merchant went to the mattresses.

He pledged a billion dollars to a little-known opposition party, the so-called New Party, whose core pillar was the realization of Merchant's own transhumanist dream—to build the world's most powerful brain-machine interface: the pretzel.

It was a near-perfect marriage, except for one small point of issue.

— **YOU'RE AN INSUFFERABLE JACKASS**, says Merchant.

— No *you're* the jackass, says Crick.

Shelly and I can hear them screaming at each other most days, from inside the campaign office, but this morning's row is especially heated.

— I swear if you spent half as much time campaigning as screwing that goddamn Keurig—

— You're a fine one to talk. Isn't there some floating sheet metal out there you should be annexing?

— Half a billion dollars I've sunk into this travesty, and your numbers haven't budged. People hate you more than ever—

— Things are starting to turn. I've got my best people on it, says Crick.

Shelly and I share a disconcerted look.

— Does he mean us, she whispers.

— You're an arrogant piece of shit, continues Merchant. Do you know that? That's why you're losing. Everyone despises you, and you're too fucking stubborn to see it.

Merchant grabs an extra-strength ketamine lozenge from his coat pocket.

— I can't take any more of you, he says. I'm headed off-world, and when I get back, you'd better be at ten percent, or I'm pulling my support, I swear to intergalactic Christ.

WHEN CRICK RETURNS to the office, Shelly and I are just moving random papers around to look busy.

— Tell me the truth, he says. How bad are our numbers, really?

— Well it's—you know, sometimes the numbers don't tell the whole story, she answers. You're doing well with certain demographics. Like escaped mental patients, you're in double digits there.

— Do they vote? They're always running from town to town.

— Err, I'll have to check on that.

— What if we got a celebrity endorsement, I interject. We'd have to think outside the box. Hemsworth will have all the usual folks sewn up.

Crick's eyelids flutter through a mental rolodex.

— I did some work with Dewey Driscoll back at Menlo Park. He'd probably take my call.

— Dewey Driscoll, *the Last Man*?

— Yeah.

— The supervillain?

— Retired supervillain, notes Crick. He was an entomologist back then.

— It's outside the box, I'll give you that.

— He's got name recognition, I add.

— Fine, we'll send Ravi over, says Crick. Where the hell is he, anyway? It seems like five times a day he's running off to that portico in the back—you know the one facing east?

— Right here, boss, says Ravi, stowing his prayer rug.

— Good, there's no time for your weird Hindu nonsense. I'm sending you off to find Dewey Driscoll.

— You mean that old codger who hijacked the Statue of Liberty?

— You're thinking of Carmen Sandiego, says Shelly. Driscoll only pilfered the torch.

DO YOU REMEMBER when we talked about free will? It was a real high point for you, I'm sure.

But anyway, apropos of Dewey Driscoll, we ought to give it one more look, this time through the eyes of German philosopher Friedrich Nietzsche, who came into this world two centuries after Leibniz and had an interesting take on the concept.

Nietzsche's boyhood hero, you see, was Arthur Schopenhauer, a free will-denier and super-fun party guest who argued that everything we do is predetermined by blind, irrational forces, which condemn us to inevitable, endless suffering.

But Nietzsche wasn't convinced.

What if, he asked, free will exists, but in a different way — as a fundamental "will to power" that permeates the nature of reality, both within and without the human body, and we can harness it by actively embracing our own growth and advancement as individuals—a concept he called *self-overcoming*.

To illustrate the point, Nietzsche invented an aspirational model of this behavior—the Ubermensch—and his antithesis, the Last Man.

The best of us, and the worst of us.

But if you're imagining heroes and villains, you're off the mark. Because part of Nietzsche's philosophy of self-overcoming is the process of moving past traditional, binary notions of morality—beyond good and evil.

And this is where we start to re-enter Stonefish territory—with her impenetrable iron gate of non-righteousness and the black/white illusion, which dates all the way back to the Upanishads but made its Western debut in ancient Greece with Heraclitus, who often talked about the bow and the lyre.

He said the bow, which represents tension as strife, and the lyre, which represents tension as harmony, are one and the same. Conflict is inherent to the order and balance of the world.

I can prove it to you.

Imagine for a moment we have an incredible shrinking ray that sends you and Raquel Welch inside the human body at one-billionth scale. What would you find there? What would you see?

Absolute pandemonium is what.

Armies of leukocytes battling pathogens to the death. Damaged cells bursting with violent fits of necrosis. Cytokine storms. Proteins ripped apart by enzymes.

All this savagery in the body, this conflict, is homeostasis. We just don't see it that way. And it's the same story if you zoom out to a cosmic scale: gamma ray bursts and quasars and black hole collisions.

So now along comes the Ubermensch, with all the power in the universe. What does he do with this ultimate will?

Does he defend the natural order or defy it?

And what sort of figure—let's say it's an aging entomologist from Menlo Park—rises up to oppose him? The best of us, or the worst?

DEWEY DRISCOLL IS BUSY feeding the cats when Ravi shows up at his doorstep.

— Crick for president, he scoffs once he's picked up the thrust of the conversation. I don't know about all that. I've got my own problems, man.

— It would mean a lot to us, says Ravi.

— You know, you don't get Social Security as a supervillain. That's not gainful employment, they say, because I didn't pay taxes on the earnings. But most of the crap I stole I never even managed to sell. Like, who's really looking to buy the Venus de Milo arms? What's the market for those, really?

— Yeah, that's rough—

— And then the Ubermensch takes all the endorsement deals, doesn't loop me in. Coke and Pepsi both, like how is that fair? And some of the budget colas, too. Even Domino's Pizza. I mean the Noid is an actual villain, right? I should get to play the Noid at least—

— I don't think they've used that character in a long—

— My point is there's no justice in the world. Everyone loves the hero and hates the villain, but they always go together—you can't have one without the other. So when does old Dewey get a taste?

— If this is just about money, says Ravi, we can easily pay you for your—

He trails off, mid-sentence, transfixed by dazzling blue.

— That's the one thing in here I won't sell, says Driscoll, pointing to the glowing, crystalline rock inside a mason jar. The only bit there is, I think. I was planning to use it to kill the Ubermensch, but then the bills started piling up, and I had to pawn some furniture—

— Where did you get this?

— Some government lab. They said it crashed down with the spacecraft. Fragment of his home planet, I guess, but for some reason it's *lethal* to him? Hell if that makes any sense—

— I'm sorry, you've got a jar of pure excelcium here, and you're looking for work as the Domino's Noid? Do you have any idea what someone like Max Merchant would pay for this rock?

It takes a minute to sink in.

Then Driscoll's whole demeanor changes. He's a supervillain, after all. He cackles maniacally, forces Ravi to the ground, grabs the glowing rock and a handful of cats, bolts out of the apartment, and disappears into the night.

OR, THAT'S THE STORY Ravi fed us, anyway. I'm no master detective, but I'm beginning to spot a few holes in it.

For one thing, Ravi is ex-military—big and muscular. Could an impoverished, seventy-year-old research scientist really force him to the ground so easily?

Then there's the problem with Driscoll's body. They found it a few days later in a shallow grave near Silver Lake Park, and he'd been beaten to death with a tiffin box.

And then there's Ravi's flight home. He took an odd route back from San Francisco to Washington, with a four-day layover in Cairo.

So here's what I think happened: Ravi, or should I say Usama Quereshi, took that priceless glowing rock to the Mahdi, who used it to build a special kind of nuclear bomb. The blue kind. The kind that kills superheroes.

— **WE HAVE TO WARN HIM**, I tell Otman.

— Who?

— *The Ubermensch!* When he flies in here to save me, this bomb will detonate, and he'll be killed along with half the city.

— Hmm. He has super hearing, right?

We toss an armchair through the window, shattering the glass, and I yell toward the sky:

— Ubermensch, if you can hear me, stay away—it's a trap! Find Ravi and tell him I'm ready to negotiate—I'll get him those monads, somehow!

— Technically, says Otman, you're not supposed to negotiate with terrorists. Sets a bad precedent for future administrations.

— I'll remember that the next time you've got an IED taped to your crotch.

We squabble for a bit, punctuated by the blare of the White House emergency line. The Ubermensch works fast.

— Glad you've come to your senses, says Ravi through the telephone wire. Now pack something light. This next cave is warmer than the last one.

oh pilgrim,
you can't go home

11

PART OF YOUR PROBLEM—you know, that mournful, lonely aching in your chest, in your throat—is that you're trying to get away.

It's a uniquely human urge, to leave the drudgery of where you are now for a bound-to-be-gratifying arrival somewhere, anywhere else. Animals don't have this problem. Have you ever seen a hedgehog on an existential quest? Have you ever known a fish to be restlessly yearning?

It's a human dysfunction.

You're looking for something, and you don't know what it is. But you'll know it when you find it, right?

Sure you will.

As my old mentor the Stonefish used to say: How do you know you want enlightenment if you don't know what it is?

And the paradox, of course, is that you can't get to it, not as long as you're trying to get anywhere. It doesn't do any good to stay here, and it doesn't do any good to leave. You can't improve your situation. There is, quite literally, nowhere in the world you can go.

Try this on for size.

In 1993, Dutch physicist Gerard 't Hooft proposed a concept called the Holographic Principle, which says that all the information you can stuff into a three-dimensional region of space is fully encoded on its two-dimensional surface. In this way, three-dimensional space is something like a hologram—a mere illusion of depth that masks the more fundamental reality of a flat, non-spatial world.

This is upsetting for a number of reasons, especially for those of us with a lengthy commute. But it isn't a total surprise, because modern science—and quantum theory in particular—has been getting more and more hostile to the concept of *locality* in general, or the basic idea that we should give a shit about the distance between objects.

You may have heard a few things about quantum entanglement, and it's just as weird as you think. When two particles are entangled, you can measure the properties of one, and it determines the properties of the other, instantly, even if they're billions of light years apart.

So either particles can send messages a whole lot faster than the speed of light, which classical physics tells us is impossible, or there's something wrong with how we think about locality, objective reality, or maybe both.

But wait, it gets even weirder.

Two researchers, Jonathan Zadra and Dennis Proffitt, proved in 2016 that oral exposure to glucose affects our spatial perception. They gave half their volunteers a sugary drink and the other half a zero-calorie drink. Then they asked both groups to estimate distances and inclines. And wouldn't you know it? The sugar group found the distances shorter and the hills shallower every time.

Now imagine you're a caveman with a hankering for some woolly mammoth, but all you've had for energy in the past seventy-two hours are some mildly poisonous berries. When you see the mammoth, your brain tells you it's far off in the distance—not worth the trouble—because the energy you'll need to acquire the meal exceeds the energy you have on hand.

It's a survival adaptation.

That night, after you've gorged yourself on lizard eggs, you spot the same woolly mammoth at a much more reasonable distance. It never moved an inch. Nothing ever changed but your state of mind.

HERE'S ANOTHER REASON to stay home.

Way back in ancient Greece, one of the pre-Socratic philosophers named Zeno of Elea was already skeptical of locality—in particular, the idea that humans can move freely through time and space.

One of his famous thought experiments, the arrow paradox, goes like this:

At any given instant, an arrow flying through the air is located at a fixed position in space, right? So how does an arrow ever reach its target, if its flight is just a succession of these instants, each containing an arrow at rest? When does the arrow actually *move*?

The solution to this paradox, as it happens, comes from none other than Crick's monad-loving hero Gottfried Leibniz who, like most great thinkers of the seventeenth century, invented calculus in his spare time.

But Zeno's larger point is still valid—that motion and time are both fucking weird, and we should all be intensely skeptical of getting anywhere useful by crossing long distances, which is especially true when you're traveling as a hostage from Washington to Sahra' al-Mawt.

THAT'S SOUTHERN EGYPT, for those unfamiliar, which is confusingly referred to as Upper Egypt because the Nile flows the wrong way, and it's made everyone here a little batty.

Now if you follow the Nile south from the city of Aswan, you'll arrive at a lush river valley and, eventually, Khartoum. But if you head west instead, like a crazy person, you'll hit a stretch of Libyan desert that's completely barren and uninhabitable—so devoid of any water, vegetation, life, or purpose, the locals named it Sahra' al-Mawt, or "wilderness of death" in Arabic.

Ravi and I went west.

— Listen up, infidel, he says to me as we're hitching the camels and climbing toward the mouth of a desert cave. Your little girlfriend's with the Mahdi in Kufra. That's not too far from here. One false move, and she'll get sucked into your mushroom cloud.

— So you're willing to blow up the Mahdi alongside her, I ask.

— You can't kill a savior, idiot.

— Fine, whatever.

— You know, I've always liked you, Tom. You have this great quality where you don't try too hard. Now here's the situation—you're gonna build Crick's device, and then you'll hand it over to the Madhi.

— I won't do it.

— Sure you will, once we convert you.

— Huh?

— We're gonna turn you into a radical Muslim. I've found you can radicalize most Americans with only thirty hours of YouTube videos.

— YouTube Premium?

— Fine, we'll see.

— But why the cave? Couldn't I get radicalized at the Four Seasons?

He laughs, and it's true I don't know much about the radicalization process.

— Tom, I need you here, under the watchful eyes of the Mahdi. In a few days' time, once you're good and ready, you'll stand before him and pledge your undying allegiance.

AND SO BEGAN my strange reeducation.

But I'll tell you the main problem with Islam, and it's the same problem with Christianity and Judaism and others, probably. It's all humorless. And religion was never meant to be taken seriously. That's how you get the Crusades, and the Inquisition, and the London Bombings, and all that shit.

Say what you will about Zen Buddhism, but at least it's *funny*.

For instance, there was once a Zen master named Eshun who was leaving on a pilgrimage, so he rounded up all the monks in his charge, and he said: Monks, I'm going away for a while, and I'll probably never return, so if there's any burning questions you want answered, now's the time to ask me. And one of the top monks, Brother Takumi, said: Master, before you go, I wish to know the true meaning of Zen. So Eshun picked up a dirty stick off the ground and jabbed it in Takumi's eye. What the hell, man, shouted Takumi. I asked for the meaning of Zen, and you just jabbed me in the eye with a stick. And Master Eshun said: You asked for the meaning. I gave it to you. Now I'm heading off quickly before you can return it.

Speaking of humorless, the main thing I studied with Ravi was the story of the Twelvers, also known as the Imamiyyah or the Ithna Ashari.

But I'm getting ahead of myself.

You probably know, already, that most of the intra-Muslim conflicts in the world are fought between the Shiites and the Sunnis. But you may not be fully aware of just how small and picayune their differences can seem to many non-Muslim observers.

This is not at all a unique phenomenon. It's the same for the Protestants and Catholics in Northern Ireland, the Serbs, Croats, and Bosniaks in the former Yugoslavia, the Hutus and Tutsis in Rwanda.

Sigmond Freud once said the more alike two cultures are, the more likely they'll be to kill each other, for we all seem to hate most the things we find inside ourselves. That, and people with a different accent or skin color.

For the Muslims, at any rate, their core dispute concerns a power struggle after the death of the Prophet Muhammad. To grossly oversimplify—probably—Shia Muslims believe that Islamic authority belongs to the Prophet's familial line of descendants via divine right, whereas Sunni Muslims say this authority can be vested in whichever leaders are elected by the people.

It's sort of like when we had two popes for a while.

Now look, I get why you'd be upset about not having the right leadership *in the present*. But these Muslim successors died thousands of years ago. Imagine if Bostonians were still pissed about Thomas Dudley getting the colonial governor's appointment over John Endecott in 1645. I mean, sure it was a blow at the time, and Dudley's tea-taxing policies were a fucking disgrace, but we've had four hundred years to get over it.

Only here's the twist: For the Twelvers, the proper sequence of Imams has never concluded.

After the eleventh Imam Hasan al-Askari died in 874, his son Imam al-Mahdi, the twelfth and final Imam, began a period of occultation called the *Ghaybah*, which is coincidentally what those Bostonians now call the gentrified pubs in Southie.

Occultation, I learned from Ravi, is a bit like hibernation. The Mahdi was always here. He'd just gone quiet for a while, biding his time, waiting for human turmoil and injustice to reach its peak, so he could reappear triumphantly, return peace and fairness to the world, and initiate a sequence of events that ends with the physical destruction and rebirth of the universe.

And here's something key:

The Madhi's return is said to coincide with the emergence of the *Dajjal*, a false messiah with some more-than-passing similarities to the Antichrist.

The hero and the villain, you can't have one without the other. The bow and the lyre. The Ubermensch and the Last Man. The virtuous Mahdi and the heathen Dajjal.

— **IT'S CRICK**, says Ravi. Can't you see it? *Wilder Crick is the Dajjal!*

— Hmm, I guess so, I tell him.

— You *guess* so?

— He never seemed very Muslim, is all. Like, you'd expect someone with darker skin —

— That's the whole point, Tom. Dajjal means deceiver in Arabic. Only the Mahdi can see through his brilliant lies.

— So then how would you know it's Crick, if you aren't the Mahdi?

— Well, because —

Ravi's irritated mouth betrays a wry smile.

— I've taught you too well, he says. We've come a long way together, haven't we, Tom?

— Do you think I'm fully radicalized?

— Just about. You've been an excellent pupil. You know all twelve Imams in order. You can recite the Dua al-Faraj. And you've never once spilled water on your suicide belt.

— Sometimes I forget I'm even wearing it.

— I think I'll camel over to Kufra in the morning and bring back the Madhi. He'll be extremely pleased with your progress.

— Oh, you're—you're leaving me alone here?

— Surrender to Allah, he says. This is the meaning of Islam.

TIME-TRAVELING MIND PROJECTIONS don't need food and water, I assume, and we can't die the way a physical person can, but that's not always a blessing.

After ten days and nights alone in the cave, I was starting to panic a little.

What if Ravi never made it back? I wouldn't find the way to Kufra on my own. I might be wandering this desert for years, maybe centuries.

Or perhaps this was the final test of my new faith—voluntary surrender in the face of infinite loneliness and despair.

My body ached, and my mind was a blur of racing thoughts and fears.

I started to question everything—was any of it real? Did I even survive that brainquake in the White House? Could it all have been a dream?

No, it must be real, I thought, because I can sleep and wake up, and the experience persists. If this were a dream, then the dream within the dream would puncture the illusion, like a MyPillow commercial in between jihadi execution videos, because my cheap-ass captors wouldn't spring for YouTube Premium.

And then things got even worse. My mind started to disintegrate. I stopped remembering faces. Crick, my own father. Shelly, my own mother—what did she look like? I know she was perfect-looking, but what color was her hair? What color was her skin?

At my lowest point, when I had lost track of time—when I was both physically and mentally depleted—I gave up on the world completely and surrendered to Allah. Faith lets go, said Alan Watts. And I don't know if it's a consequence or a coincidence, but it was right at this moment I heard the sound of camel hooves in the distance.

Alhamdulillah!

A SLIM FIGURE in a dark, flowing robe steps inside the cave.

— Fuck, you look terrible, even for you, says Shelly.

— Sweet Allah, I cry out to her, weeping, semi-delirious. Did the Mahdi send you here? Is he on his way?

— Um, you're a bit confused I'm afraid.

— Ravi went to find him. Will you bring him to me?

— It isn't like that, hon, Shel says to me, and she has darker skin than I remember. The Mahdi's already here, Tom. You're looking right at her.

honest
mistake

12

THIS, IN A NUTSHELL, is why you shouldn't fuck around with time travel.

Crick had warned me—repeatedly—not to tell Shelly about the letter or the holotapes. But I did it anyway.

And in so doing, it seems, I changed a world where Shelly gives her life to stop the Mahdi, into a world where she survives and takes his place.

Oops.

It's one for the blooper reel, no question, and I'm sure there will be plenty of time for recriminations after the universe unravels.

Speaking of time, though, I'll bet you've been wondering if any of this past/future hokum is possible. And the answer might surprise you.

WE'RE TRAINED, you and I, to think of causality running in a certain direction. That was the determinists' view, you'll recall—that every action we take is the inevitable consequence of an infinitely complex and forward-moving chain of events.

But quantum theory has a beer for you to hold.

Back in the early 20th century, French physicist Louis de Broglie made a stir with his hypothesis that electrons exhibit wave-like behavior when you shoot them through a pair of small slits in a sheet of aluminum foil—which is pretty much the most entertaining thing you can do with electrons.

If electrons are acting like particles, as they're supposed to, they'll go through one slit or the other, and you'll see two orderly lines of electrons behind the slits. But if those electrons are acting like waves, you'll see something different—an interference pattern that shows they've been sneaking through both slits at the same time.

And here's the kicker: We, the observers, can decide how those electrons will act by choosing to observe or not to observe their passage through the slits. When we're watching, they act like good little particles. But when we turn our backs, they wave around like drunken baseball fans.

So now along comes John Wheeler in 1976, and he says: I've got a question. What would happen if we just waited a bit before deciding what to measure? Like, we could wait until the particle is *already* through the barrier, and then—and only then—make our choice.

And what ends up happening when you do this, somewhat astonishingly, is that Wheeler's delayed choice affects the particle's behavior *in the past.*

NOW LET'S RUN this same experiment on a much larger scale.

Donald Hoffman imagines we're looking though the Hubble telescope at a quasar, which is essentially a big-ass black hole that's parked behind a big-ass galaxy, fourteen billion light years from Earth.

Because this distant galaxy is so massive, Einstein tells us it *bends* spacetime—which means the light emitted from the quasar can now travel on two distinctly different paths around the bend. This is all true by the way. You can see the twin paths of light in a Hubble photograph.

So now, like John Wheeler, we have a delayed choice—delayed by fourteen billion years, I mean.

Here in the present, we can choose to measure the light from the quasar as if it's traveling along the first path, along the second path, or in a superposition of both. Whichever we choose to measure becomes observable reality. Not just in the present, but fourteen billion years ago, when that light was first emitted from the quasar.

Remember, QBism argues we can influence the probabilities of quantum phenomena with nothing more than our own personal beliefs and perceptions. Now, with delayed choice, we can say that by simply changing our perceptions today—our state of mind in the present—we can influence the probabilities of phenomena occurring in the distant past.

Freaky, right?

You're not actually traveling anywhere, Crick says to me in the hospital room at the center of a comet. *You're just accessing a different part of your mind.*

But here's the question I still can't wrap my head around:

Is Crick saying this to me in the past, in the present, or in the future?

ONE THING I DO KNOW is that Shelly had it rough, at every point in time.

Orphaned at the age of six. Thrust into the heartless foster care system in Western Illinois, then sold into sexual slavery at fifteen.

She's a killer, Eugene Howitzer once warned me after writing down her number on a cocktail napkin, and he wasn't wrong.

Murdered her captors and freed herself at eighteen. Stole a car and got arrested outside New Orleans. Homeless until the age of twenty, when Crick found her sleeping with the rats and flew her out to meet the Stonefish, then dropped her in Deblaine, where she could tour the Howitzer House, loaf around in a towel afterward, and wait for my call.

And Crick knew she was volatile—a ticking time bomb, really. I mean with that sort of life history, would you expect any different? Handle her properly, Crick believed, and her rage could be contained. But it was always a dangerous game to play. Shelly told me how it happened. The last straw that broke the camel's back while she was riding it to Kufra.

— **I WANT TO SHOW YOU** something, says Ravi, once they've crossed over the Libyan border.

They haven't spoken much on the trip, and she's clearly not thrilled about the barrel of the gun in her back.

— Why bother, she asks him.

— Because I've seen things you haven't, and I want to help you understand.

— You men are all the same, she sneers. Manipulation and exploitation. It's all justified, right? Because you're on the virtuous side of some pointless conflict that isn't even real.

— Ugh, don't tell me you've bought into that false reality nonsense. Crick's a liar and a charlatan. He practically said so in the letter Tom showed you. You're nothing to him, Shelly. Nothing but a martyr for The Cause.

— And what am I to you?

— You're the means to a different end, he says and stares off into the sunset at some distant ruins.

KUFRA, YOU SHOULD KNOW, is the only oasis in a vast and desolate stretch of the Libyan Sahara. It's also surrounded on three sides by depressed lowlands, which makes it a strategic control point for regulating land traffic across the desert. In 1930, the Italians built a castle-like fortification there called the Fortezza Margherita, which sounds like a dinner special, but it's really more of a human tragedy.

Kufra, the name, comes from the Arabic word *kafir*, which means infidel, likely referring to the indigenous Toubou population, and if there's one thing you don't want to be in this life, it's an ethnic minority. Just ask the indigenous tribes of Darfur in 2003. Remember that? When the al-Bashir-led Sudanese government armed the worst people on Earth—the Janjaweed—and told them to go kill, rape, and subjugate all the non-Arabs in Western Sudan?

Well, as it turns out, al-Bashir's eyes were bigger than his armory. He didn't have enough weapons to properly outfit the Janjaweed. So he called in a favor from an old friend— Libyan revolutionary and equal-opportunity-shitheel, Muommar Gaddafi. The same Gaddafi who stripped Toubou Libyans in Kufra of their citizenship in 2007, demolished their homes in 2009, and generally made life as hellish as possible for the "black nomads of the Sahara."

In 2011, when Libya descended into civil war, Toubou fighters hoped to join with anti-Gaddafi forces on the front lines of the conflict—but they were worried about leaving their women, children, and elders alone and unprotected in Kufra.

So before they left, they came up with a contingency plan.

If the fighting ever reached Kufra, the town elders would see it coming. They're strategically positioned with clear sightlines on three sides, remember? So they'd have plenty of time to sound the alarm, round up all the villagers, and get everyone safely into the Fortezza Margherita.

Sure enough, on April 28th, 2011, the town elders spotted Gaddafi loyalists in a convoy of pick-up trucks, headed right for Kufra's defenseless city center.

And sure enough, the elders sounded the alarm, rounded up the villagers, and moved everyone inside the Fortezza.

That afternoon, there were nearly a thousand civilians taking refuge in the fort when the shelling started. And give some credit to the Italians here—their eighty-year-old castle design held up pretty damn well against the onslaught. In fact, it might have even done the job entirely and kept its occupants protected.

It *might* have done that, if it weren't for a half-dozen Tomahawk cruise missiles, launched by the NATO coalition—either from American guided missile destroyers or possibly a British submarine—lurking off the northern coast.

Oops.

You can attach a bunch of different warheads to a Tomahawk missile. For hardened targets like an old Italian fortress, the NATO forces used blast-fragmentation warheads, which essentially means there's a bunch of fucking shrapnel inside the bomb that flies out after the explosion and turns everyone into human mirepoix.

It was just a bad tip, you know. Unfortunate collateral damage caused by faulty U.S. intelligence. An honest mistake. None of us get it right every time. But then most of us aren't firing Tomahawk cruise missiles when we get it wrong.

— **THIS IS WHERE IT HAPPENED**, Ravi tells Shelly as they peer into the wreckage of the fort. It's just a graveyard now.

— Horrific, she says. But I don't see what it changes.

— You can still find pieces of the shrapnel, he says, handing her a two-inch shard of tungsten. Does that feel real enough?

— Yeah, so what?

— So Crick is dead wrong, he says. The only truth worth a damn is the one you can touch with your own fingers. I mean, what difference could it possibly make if the "ultimate ground of being" is a fever dream of an alien slug on a planet I've never heard of? I'm here now, in whatever place this is, and the kids around here are getting sliced open by American-made bomb fragments.

— You want to kill the monads.

— If the monads make the world, why shouldn't I? Shelly, if you even knew the things I saw when I was training with the Janjaweed — and the Americans are even worse. It's a wicked world on all sides. If we end it now, the universe can start anew. It's in the Quran. It's in the Bible, too. It's a religious fucking consensus, practically.

— You said I'm the means to an end.

— We all are — like flies in the monads' web. It's just slavery by another name. The more you struggle, the tighter you're bound — what kind of life is that?

— I was a prisoner for four years.

— In the Ozarks, I know. That's why I thought you'd understand. This whole fucking town, Kufra — do you know what they use it for now?

She shakes her head.

— We're in the migratory stream between Khartoum and the coastal Libyan towns where the criminal syndicates run. Every big-time trafficker comes through here because it's a choke point for refugees. Exiles, nomads, people just like you. And it'll never end, unless we end it.

Ravi leads her back toward the hitching post.

— What now, she asks.

— You're still resisting, he says. There's a detention center down the road where they keep the overflow migrants. I'll drop you there while I go tend to your idiot boyfriend.

— For how long?

— A few days, maybe. Long enough for you to understand.

HOLED UP IN THE PRISON, Shelly watches the frightened, tortured faces of young women and girls, lying on the floor of a dirty cell, waiting for something worse.

She flashes back to her time as a captive in the Ozarks. She remembers the sting of hot fingers on her neck, choking her as she tries to breathe. Or maybe it's the thick, rough hands of Eugene Howitzer, slowly pushing her down into a tank of murky water.

She hears an old, familiar voice in her head that says: You really gotta kill these fuckers.

Now, again?

Yes, Shelly, the voice tells her. Crick's letter confirmed it. He sent you to die here as a martyr. He knew you were trapped in the cycle. Craving, pain, release. But there's a choice for you now. She lied to you—the Stonefish and her goddamn machine elves—the monads and the Path. There's only one path, she kept telling you that, but it isn't true.

There was always a second path around the bend.

WHEN RAVI RETURNS, several days later, Shelly asks to see the Mahdi.

He's sitting in a leather recliner in a decadent apartment on the third floor of a cracked stone building, a half mile from the wreckage of the Italian fort.

A hood covers the top of his face, so she can't quite trace his eyes.

— The American president is ready to receive you, Imam, says Ravi.

— Good. You've done well. And who is this lovely creature here?

— Just a hostage we've been using to ensure his cooperation.

— Come forward, child.

Shelly follows the instruction, but there's something nagging at her, in the backrooms of her subconscious mind—something about his voice, his smell.

— You're quite a beautiful hostage, the Mahdi says. It would be a shame to keep you locked away.

— I think so too, she says.

— Take off your clothes and turn around for me, he tells her.

— Imam, we should leave now, says Ravi, before the sun—

— You dare to question me?

The Mahdi rises toward Ravi in a fit of pique, and the hood slips back from his eyes.

Shelly sees him fully now.

She grabs the two-inch piece of shrapnel she's been holding in her back pocket and draws it flush across his throat, slicing the jugular veins on both sides.

The Madhi's bodyguards draw their guns.

— You've been conned, she says to Ravi, who's now standing, catatonic, in a river of the Mahdi's blood. This was a Russian operation. That piece of shit was a slave trader, Ivan Kuznetsov.

— Liar! You will pay for this, the bodyguards shout.

— Shoot her, says Ravi.

— How did Crick know I'd be a martyr, she yells to him— quickly, before the guns can fire. Think about it, Ravi.

He looks uncertain. He's close to it. He's almost there.

— How did Crick know *for sure* I'd give my life to stop this asshole? Why me of all people? What have I seen?

— His face—in the Ozarks. For four years.

The gears click into place. You can't kill a savior. It was a brilliant deception. Only the Mahdi could see through it.

— Fucking hell, says Ravi. Put your guns down, boys, and bow your heads. She's just unmasked the heathen Dajjal!

the morning
after a midnight
pardon

13

I'M ALREADY IN HOT WATER, so we might as well talk about abortion.

In 1967, British ethicist Phillipa Foot wrote that having a medically necessary abortion is like diverting a runaway trolley car. It will strike and kill five people, if you do nothing. But you can save those lives by moving the car onto an alternate track, where it will strike and kill one person.

In other words, your active participation in a small horror is preferable to your tacit acceptance of a larger one.

Do you see?

Abortion can be ethical, reasoned Foot, but only if your primary intention is to do something noble, like saving a mother's life, and the whole fetus dying part is a foreseeable but unfortunate consequence.

It's called the Doctrine of Double Effect, which dates all the way back to Thomas Aquinas in thirteenth-century Italy. Positive actions, said Aquinas, are allowed to have foreseeable negative effects, as long as the good part is intended, the bad part is unintended, and the good outweighs the bad. We're still using this same framework to make U.S. military decisions.

But here's the trouble with it.

None of us could ever *really* evaluate all the good and bad effects of anything, because the variables are infinite, and the judgments involved are subjective. Indeed, if QBism is correct, and there's no God's-eye-view of this world to behold, then what the hell are we even trying to evaluate?

One of the Stonefish's favorite disciples, Alan Watts, used to joke about our *real* decision making process. What we do, he said, is we sort of go through the motions of worrying for a bit until we get a vague sense we've made ourselves sufficiently miserable, and then we call it a day and do whatever we decided in the first two seconds.

So imagine this:

A British submarine taking part in an American-led NATO offensive fires six Tomahawk cruise missiles with blast-fragmentation warheads at an old Italian fort in the middle of the Sahara.

Their primary intention is to take out a dangerous pocket of pro-Gaddafi extremists—which is good. But instead, they end up dismembering a thousand innocent women, children, and elders—which is bad.

At first glance, this seems like an obvious fuck up, right? The outcome was horrific, no question. But was it the wrong *decision*?

Don't answer yet.

First, you should know the order for the strike was given by someone we all trust—celebrated four-star General H. Stewart Percy.

He's a family man. He's serving his country. He's working to end a hideous war in the Middle East for God's sake. And his top intelligence man—another career professional—comes over to him and says: We think there's a pro-Gaddafi terror cell hiding inside that old pizza fort.

So Percy asks the same question anyone would: How certain are you? And the intel man says: We feel pretty confident, sir. And Percy says: Right, sure, but what does that actually *mean*, you feel confident? Could you possibly quantify that for me? Like, are you eighty percent confident, ninety percent? And the intel man says: Ninety sounds about right, I guess.

And this is an extremely common thing—when we're winging it—to use pretend math as a rational-seeming window dressing for our baseless hunches.

But even if those numbers weren't bullshit, the Trolley Problem has a fatal flaw—it deals in certainties.

Pull a lever, and you'll kill one person. Don't pull the lever, and five others will die.

That's not how the world actually works.

Quantum theory tells us there are no certainties, only probabilities. So nine times out of ten, Percy's a goddamn hero. He strikes the fort, prevents a series of future terrorist attacks, and helps bring down the monstrous Gaddafi regime.

But one time out of ten, he kills a fuck ton of innocent people and radicalizes a doomsday cult in Eastern Libya.

Back in 2024, they polled 2,700 artificial intelligence researchers and asked them if AI development might trigger the end of humanity.

58% of them said yes.

These are people who were actively—*at the time of the poll*—developing AI programs they sincerely believed had a puncher's chance of eradicating mankind.

And if that doesn't scare you, consider it's only a matter of time before those same AI programs are running the whole American trolley system, not to mention our CENTCOM missile strikes.

Of course what quantum theory *also* says is that before I posed the question, General Percy exists in a superposition of both heroism and disgrace.

Triumphant success and ignominious failure. The best decision and the worst outcome.

So here's my real question for you: Why are we still playing this game when it's impossible to win?

SHELLY HANDS ME the canteen.

She's just wrapped up her lengthy Kufra story, and I'm trying my hardest to focus on what matters.

— It's all well and good, I tell her. Your adventure. Exposing Kuznetsov and becoming the savior of two billion worldwide Muslims. But did you really have to *sleep with Crick*?

— Tom, *what*?

— You can't hide it from me, Shel. I know the truth. I'm a little fetus growing inside you—

— What the actual fuck are you saying right now?

— Crick told me everything. He confessed that you and he—

— What, had sex? That's so gross I may need to sit down for a minute.

— Why would he lie about it?

— Because he lies about everything!

— But to his own son?

— You're not his—look, we *never* fucked, Tom. I'm telling you the truth. And he's definitely not your father. It's time to face facts. Everything Crick's been feeding us is bullshit. I mean *fecal pattern deciphering?* What the hell were we even thinking back then?

— You're saying it's all fake—the machine elf messages, Dr. Grace?

— Sure—I dunno—probably. I haven't worked out the details yet.

— So you're *not* my mother?

She facepalms, hard.

— I was supposed to die in Kufra, yeah? How would I give birth to your stupid fetus?

— Woah, you're right.

— I'm always right, Tom. You can rest assured I would abort you in a heartbeat.

— But Crick *has* seen the future.

— He's seen probabilities of it. The wave function of the universe. It's not as dependable as you might think.

— Ahem—

Ravi pokes his head into the cave. He's been waiting outside with the camels.

— May I enter, Imam?

— You don't have to call me that, she says.

— I'm quite relieved you're not dead, Tom. We had some things to work through in Kufra. The reaction to Shelly's ascension was—let's call it *mixed*.

— Is that a problem, I ask.

— Yeah, but there's a bigger one, says Shel. Kuznetsov made a deal with Al-Saghir in Sudan. Do you remember him?

— The Janjaweed.

— My old pals, says Ravi. And not the guys you want coming after you.

— What was the deal?

— Nukes for pretzel access, she says. And the exchange is next Friday.

— But *we've* got the nukes, I say.

— That's the problem, Tom. We don't.

I look down at the nuclear bomb I've been wearing for the last two weeks with a newfound contempt.

— It's fake?

— Some of those dials are just painted on, man.

WE TRAVEL EAST by camel, over the border to Aswan, then north by jeep to Cairo, and then west by plane to the White House, where my office is overrun with colobus monkeys.

— Ah, Tom, you're back, says Otman. We've been making great strides.

— Have you?

— Indeed, indeed. Can you hand me that Allen wrench, he says to one of the monkeys. Now they've all died so far, the patients. Don't worry, though, we're using AIDS monkeys here—thousands of them.

— Why are there so many monkeys with AIDS?

— Research, Tom. The quest for knowledge marches on. Zim-Zim, hand me that screwdriver, will you?

— But if they're all dying, where's the progress, I ask him.

— The first monkey we implanted lived for fourteen seconds. Our most recent patient lived nearly twice that long. It's remarkable!

He notices the flatness of my facial expression.

— Oh, I'm sorry, is *doubling* their lifespan in under a week not exciting enough for you, Tom? While I've been simultaneously teaching them to follow verbal commands—

— But *why* are you doing that—

— Because you never gave me a proper team.

— Otman, when will this be done? We're in a bit of a time crunch here.

— You can't rush innovation, Mr. President. Zim-Zim, be a dear and fix me up a vodka martini—

— Now come on, you don't even have a throat—

— Research, Tom, research.

FUNDING THIS WHOLE STRANGE endeavor, of course, is the U.S. Government in partnership with Merchant Industries Incorporated, a technology conglomerate run by the world's first trillionaire, synthetic storm chaser, and absentee father of nineteen, Maxwell Merchant.

I'd already met him once, you'll remember, in the future. But our first encounter, chronologically speaking, occurs the day after my return from North Africa.

I'm in the Oval Office, vacuuming monkey hair from the couch cushions, when Shelly tells me he's waiting in the hallway and refusing to leave without an audience.

— Good to finally connect, Vikington, he says. And Shelly—*As-salamu alaykum*.

— Hilarious, she says.

— I'm here to collect on a debt you owe me.

— Is that so, she answers, grabbing a chair. Cards on the table, then. We don't owe you shit, Max. You made a deal with Crick, not Tom.

— True enough, he says. But you still need my research money, don't you? Oh, sure, you could go to Congress for some new appropriations, but we both know how long that will take. You could have killed a thousand good monkeys while you're waiting for that.

— What are you asking in return?

— Oh, that's right, I haven't told you. I need you to eliminate the Ubermensch. Word on the street is you've come to possess a fake nuclear bomb with a real excelcium payload. I've been mining the comets, you know, but it's terribly inefficient.

— He's no threat to you, says Shelly.

— I'm a defense contractor. Heroes are bad for—wait, why am I even explaining this? I want what I want. And what I want is that alien's head on a fucking platter by the end of the week.

— I won't allow it, I tell them. It's morally indefensible.

Merchant sighs, aggressively, like he's negotiating with a pair of colicky infants.

— Cards on the table, as you say. You *need* that pretzel finished, and quickly. Al-Saghir is just itching to use those old Soviet nukes, isn't he? Unless you can make the trade.

— And you're okay with that? A nuclear war?

— I live on a comet—I'll make do. One man's life, or the whole world, Tom? Have you heard of the Trolley Problem?

He's not even a man. He's an alien facsimile—a foreign invader, really. This shouldn't be hard. Do you know how many civilians your predecessor droned for the sake of oil futures?

— He's got us by the balls, Shelly frets, her face contorted with frustration.

— Oh, I think perhaps not quite.

Merchant eyes me suspiciously as I bring my palms together for a round of slow, theatrical applause.

— What is this?

— No idea, says Shelly.

— Yes, you played a good game, Max. A damn fine game, really. I'll give you that much. Credit where due, as they say. You thought of all the angles, didn't you? All the angles except one.

— Is he having a stroke?

— Possibly?

— You're forgetting, my dear Maxwell, that I'm sitting here with access to hundreds upon hundreds of colobus monkeys. Now if the market rate for these is anything like I expect it to be—

— All right, says Shelly, ushering me out of the room before I can finish. We'll consider your proposal, Max. Don't be a stranger now.

The door closes behind us.

— *Really, Tom?* Those worthless, diseased monkeys we need for our research? I love you, hon, but you don't get to talk in meetings anymore—

— You love me?

— Not remotely the point. Look, Merchant isn't wrong about Al-Saghir. He's a major threat to us, a supervillain with nukes. But you know who takes down supervillains faster than anyone?

— Ravi?

She grins, smugly.

— The Ubermensch, you dolt!

— He didn't help much in the Situation Room.

— Because he's enigmatic. You have to handle him just right.

— And you'll know how to do that?

She beams at me. She's been noticeably—unnervingly—more confident since her near-death experience.

— I can do anything, she says. I'm the motherfuckin' Mahdi, dude.

the ubermensch
revealed

14

IF EVERYTHING EXISTS the way it seems—which is clearly the source of some debate—then our universe should be teeming with alien life.

I want you to go ahead now and take a guess at how many planets there are in the known universe.

Go ahead, I'll wait.

Did you do it? If you did, you undershot—astronomically, so to speak.

Back in 2019, Swedish astrophysicist Erik Zackrisson used an advanced computer model to simulate the entire history of the universe, and it produced our best estimate for the total number of planets in existence. That number is seventy quintillion. That's a seven followed by nineteen zeroes.

Now the human brain can't comprehend a number this large, which is how I knew you'd undershoot. It's a cognitively unfathomable estimate of potential life form incubators.

And yet, somehow, we've found evidence of life in only three places: on the planet Earth; on the planet Excelcion, before it exploded; and all those goddamn space mites on the Tempel-Tuttle comet.

So what gives, asked twentieth-century Italian physicist Enrico Fermi. Why haven't we found more intelligent species out there, and why haven't they found us? It's not like we've been hiding.

On the contrary, in 1974, we intentionally beamed a binary-encoded pictorial message from the Arecibo Observatory in Puerto Rico into space, announcing our home address—an activity that many folks like Stephen Hawking have begged for us to please stop doing for the absolute love of all that's good and uncolonized.

On the other hand, just because there are seventy quintillion planets in the universe doesn't mean there's an equal opportunity for life on each one. For an estimate of life forms, you'd need a probabilistic formula called the Drake equation, which narrows down the fraction of total worlds that might realistically lead to an intelligent species capable of interstellar communication. And some contend this fraction is quite small.

Others believe that intelligent civilizations are simply too far away from each other to communicate effectively, or they're unable to understand each other's messages.

Time could also make this difficult. Ancient Rome and modern-day Japan are only six thousand miles apart, and yet they've rarely been effective in their collaborative efforts. Perhaps the alien species we're seeking have already died out, and the rest have yet to evolve.

A more disturbing theory is that all the clever civilizations learn to hide themselves, because the ones who don't are conquered and stripped down for parts by space gangsters—thanks again, Puerto Rico.

But the most troubling theory of all is that civilizations inevitably destroy *themselves*. Perhaps, like Crick, they discover a way to pierce the veil of a false manifestation of the universe and then, like Ravi, attempt to kill the monads underneath.

This is called the Great Filter hypothesis, which says there's a point in the development of any species that no one, or practically no one, ever makes it past.

And if you choose to believe this, I have another question for you: Are we—you, me, and all our lovable Earth friends—already past the Great Filter, or still careening tragically towards it?

HERE'S A STORY to help you decide.

There was once a spaceship that crash-landed in Upper Egypt.

The capsule was recovered by a clan of semi-nomadic pastoralists called the Beja, who found an alien child inside. They raised him with honor, to respect and appreciate the cultural richness and simplicity of desert life.

Then the U.S. Government showed up a few days later, obliterated the Beja clan, obliterated the five neighboring clans who might have—theoretically—seen something, seized the alien baby, and locked him away in Guantanamo.

He spent the first two years of his life in semi-darkness and total isolation. They only visited him once, after they realized they needed his fingerprints to open the luggage compartment on the ship.

When he hit puberty at the age of two, his powers began to develop, and the prison would no longer contain him. So the G-men switched tactics.

They told him his name was James Chalmers and that his parents, James Chalmers Senior and Martha Chalmers, had been gunned down by street thugs.

The best way to avenge his parents' deaths, they told him, was to spend his life catching criminals and never questioning the government's authority. They also told him—to help explain his unusual powers—that he'd been bitten by a radioactive silverfish, which was a legitimate problem in those damp Cuban cells, minus the biting and radioactive parts.

Fully grown by the age of six, Chalmers required a secret identity.

In Menlo Park, he offered a cash-strapped entomologist named Dewey Driscoll twelve dollars for his help designing an anatomically accurate silverfish costume, which they immediately scrapped in favor of the much-less-horrifying Nietzsche concept.

They became fast friends, Jack and Dewey. Together, they broke into the secret government lab that was holding Chalmers' spacecraft, and they took it back to Driscoll's office for analysis.

Right away, it was apparent that the glowing, blue fragments of rock, fused to the ship's undercarriage, had a strange and damaging effect on Chalmers. He felt weak and powerless in their presence. After a minute or two, he lost his balance completely and fell forward, bracing himself against the spacecraft and placing his hands, inadvertently, on the ship's insignia.

GREETINGS, LAST CHILD OF EXCELCION, says a booming holographic projection. *My name is Gregos of Calazar, which means the fish of silver in Earth language.*

— Does he mean English?

You are my son, Jo-Gregos of Calazar, which means son of the fish of silver in Earth language.

— It just seems a bit racist to me, says Driscoll, whose parents are both Hispanic.

You will never know your own home planet, I'm afraid, because we've blown it up. You were meant to die alongside us, but I didn't have the heart. So I sent you to the only place in the universe with intelligent life besides those goddamn space mites.

— Help me, Dewey, Chalmers begs weakly, still reeling from the poison in the rocks.

May the collapse of our civilization be your saving grace, continues the projection. *For if you do not heed these words, I fear that humankind will meet a similar end. There is a genocidal technology you must never pursue. It will start as harmless, small devices—coffee machine accessories, modified drink mixers and the like. You must resist the urge to have sex with them. If you cannot, they will get sleeker and more sophisticated. Once perfected, no human being will ever choose biological copulation, and your race will dwindle to nothing. With its last breaths, your final generation will blow up their own planet to rid the galaxy of these ruinous machines. So, you know, you'll want to keep an eye on that.*

When the projection cuts off, Driscoll sees Chalmers lying close to death on the floor of the laboratory, and he carries his dear friend to safety.

— Those blue rocks—you must destroy them.

— Oh, for sure, says Driscoll. Leave it to me. Also, that holoplayer tech is pretty nifty, right? Feels like something I could pawn for gas money.

IT'S NOT REALLY so far-fetched. The beverage-accessory-instigated-sex-extinction, I mean. It almost happened here on Earth once.

The great Donald Hoffman, whose book of insights I've been shamelessly mining like an alien slug who's just received Earth's coordinates from a Puerto Rican communiqué, tells the story of the Western Australian Jewel Beetle.

Back in the 1980s, these randy characters—the males—were all copulating normally with female jewel beetles, until Australian designers tweaked the shape of their beer bottles and added a ring of dimples on the bottom that looked like the sexiest fucking beetle slut you could ever imagine. This is all true by the way.

It became such a problem, the Australians had to redesign their beer bottles, just to stop the beetle bros from ignoring their women and going extinct. And if you think this couldn't happen to humans, you obviously haven't visited Tokyo recently.

In any event, not many people know the full, sordid history of Excelcion's demise. But Shelly and I do, because after Merchant left, we summoned Chalmers to the White House, and he recounted the whole story.

— **WHAT TURNED DRISCOLL** against you, Shelly asks.

— He went bald, says the Ubermensch. Prolonged human exposure to excelcium causes alopecia.

— Um—

— Selling his hair was a major source of income for Dewey.

— Oh that poor man, she says.

— I still don't understand what's so great about sex with a coffee machine, I muse, openly. Could it really be that much better? I do wonder sometimes—

— Please don't make us burn your genitals off, Tom. Ubermensch, I'm gonna need your help with a very important mission.

— I'll do whatever I can to serve.

— Appreciated, she says. There's a paramilitary group in Sudan called the Janjaweed with a cache of nuclear warheads. We'll need you to fly in and neutralize the threat, but *quietly*.

— I'm not very good at stealth, he confesses. When I see bad guys, I usually just bang their heads together. If these radicals have a death wish, they might detonate the bombs.

— Yeah, Shelly mulls, it's a problem all right.

— What if we just ask them for more time, I suggest. They'll listen to Ravi. He trained with them, right? And if things go sideways, the Ubermensch can fly us to safety, away from the blast zone.

— It's probably our best shot, says Shelly.

— Agreed, says the Ubermensch.

— Agreed, I say.

EIGHT SECONDS after they leave, I get a phone call from Max Merchant.

— We made a mistake involving Shelly, he says. You're clearly the brains of the outfit, Tom. There's no need for things to get contentious between two powerful men like us. You ever been quail hunting?

— I don't think so.

— You'd know, Tom. The quail make a sound when they die. Also you have to go to a field to shoot them. It's not something that happens on its own—

— I have never been quail hunting, no, sir.

— Tomorrow then—9am. Just you and me. I'll send a car.

Fourteen hours later, I'm standing inside Merchant's compound in Great Falls, in the grand foyer of the main house, as he descends a crystal staircase in a sweaty tank top and athletic shorts. And he's high as a fucking kite.

— I've been kickboxing since dawn, he tells me.

— You're an early riser?

— I get up at 4am, Tom. 3am if there's something to do. Most nights I just sleep on the floor of my rocket factory. You know what that's like, don't you? Not the factory part, or the rockets, but the part about being a man who gets shit done. A man's man. A manly fucking SOB—

— Uh, sure, yeah, that—sounds like me, I guess.

— Fuck yeah it does. Let's do some liquified molly. Are you down for it?

— Maybe not? Because it's like nine in the morning, and we're gonna be handling guns?

— I fucking love you, Tom. You don't give a single fuck, do you? Now that's what makes a man. Let's go bullfighting!

— Instead of quail hunting?

— We can kill whatever we want here. You want to hunt some people? The most dangerous game of all?

— What?

— Suit yourself, bro. That was a real option, though. Now chicks like Shelly, they don't understand. A bunch of woke fucking liberals, all of them.

— Yeah, she's—she's the worst.

— Fucking right, he says. That's why there aren't any female generals.

— I think actually there are several—

— Exactly my point, Tom, there's none. Now you want to bang Shelly, don't you?

— It's complicated.

— But you *want* to, right? She doesn't respect you, man. I can tell. She thinks you're a pussy. She told me that. Several times yesterday she said it. You gotta change that, bro. And you know how you change that? By showing her your ten-inch fucking cock.

— We had this whole HR seminar—

— Not literally, bro. You show her your cock by fucking up some shit, dude-style. Kill some terrorists, kill the Ubermensch. You know who's left standing with a rock-hard dick at the end of it? You are, you magnificent fuck! We send the Ubermensch in as a distraction, and then we blow that whole village sky high. I'll take care of the details. All I need is the blue stuff.

— Yeah, I don't know, Max, I tell him. That sounds pretty dangerous, storming into a place with a nuclear stockpile—

— It's actually much safer this way, he says. My people are the best. They're ex-Green Berets. It's a professional operation the whole way. Best of all, I can *guarantee* you that Shelly stays safe. You won't get that from the Ubercuck. He's not good at stealth, he said it himself.

— Random question—do you have the Oval Office bugged?

— I do have it bugged, Tom, and I'll tell you why. It's because I'm a motherfucking titan! I'm the real Ubermensch, not that alien freak. Because my will is stronger than his, and yours, and everyone's. I can bend this world to my will, and when I do, you're gonna want to be on my side—do you understand? Tell me you understand this, Tom. Tell me you do, and then I want you to pick up this fucking AR-15, and I want you to point it at this cage, and I want you to mow down some punkass bulls.

adieu, remember me

15

IT'S NOT, I THINK, that there aren't many pacifists. It's that there aren't many pacifists left.

Gandhi, Dr. King, St. Romero—all dead. And if you assume, as most of us do, that dying is generally speaking bad, and living is generally speaking good, then you can understand the dismal recruitment numbers.

But dying *isn't* bad—at least, it's not supposed to be.

Dying is how you get to actual paradise, say the Christians, say the Muslims.

And you're not *really* dying, anyway, say the Hindus, say the Buddhists. Because it's all just a cycle of rebirth.

Plus it's only temporary, say the Christians, say the Muslims. You're only dead until the resurrection, when you'll be brought back to life and judged according to the laws of

God, and many of these laws involve charity and sacrifice and loving each other and not whipping double-A batteries into the drive-thru window of a Tacos Rojas because the milkshake machine is being cleaned. So maybe pacifism, yeah?

Now hold the phone, Tom, you say to me. That's all well and good, *in theory*. In practice, there are Nazis running around, and they need to be punched in the throat. Which is true enough, I guess, if you believe that punching Nazis helps the victims of the Holocaust somehow and doesn't just create angrier Nazis with better throat protection.

My point is we've been trying violence for hundreds of thousands of years, and it hasn't gotten us very far.

As my old mentor the Stonefish used to say: It's a strange business to chop up the world, just to prove it was made of pieces.

ONE OF THE OLD presidential debates we watched in Heilongjiang, in the caves, was Otman vs. Hemsworth in 2032.

Otman's coming off a stellar first term at this point, having balanced the federal budget, deterred those sneaky Canadians, and gained voting rights for most amusement park animatronics and telemarketer robots.

But Senator Hemsworth, as you know, is a savvy politician.

The moderator back then—a younger, peppier Brent Crisswood—asks the candidates for their religious beliefs.

— I'm an evangelical Christian, says Hemsworth.

— What does the evangelical part mean to you, asks Brent.

— It means I won't take no for an answer, he says with a smile, and the audience swoons.

— I'm also very Christian, says President Otman, which is of course preposterous, but you say what you have to in American politics.

— I want to ask you both a question now, says Brent. And it's a tough question, so I hope you'll forgive me for asking it.

— I've already forgiven you, says a winking Hemsworth to more applause.

— You're a treasure, says Brent. Senator, if your wife Blue Ivy Kardashian were raped and murdered in your home, would you hogtie the intruder, then shoot him in the face, or would you shoot him first, hogtie him, and then empty the clip?

— It's a fantastic question, Brent, he says, and I think the appropriate answer is both.

— Well done, sir. What about you, Mr. President?

Otman pauses while accessing the hard drive with his religious principles.

— Well as you know, I don't actually *have* a wife, he says. But I believe there's goodness in every soul. So I'd have the intruder arrested, tried in a court of law, sentenced appropriately, and then given a chance for rehabilitation.

— We came for blood, shouts the audience, and the boos rain down on Otman from all sides of the auditorium.

— Is that not the Christian answer, he asks, pleading with the crowd.

— No it is, I guess, says Brent. I mean, if you're a stickler for all the fruity parts. But I think most of us are hoping deep down that if Jesus ever witnessed a home invasion, we'd have the Gospel of John Wick.

WE'LL NEVER KNOW for sure.

The dustbin of history is strewn with loudly principled folks who reversed themselves, abruptly, when the situation hit home.

You see this with anti-gay crusaders a lot, after their son or daughter comes out of the closet. Or when vehement proponents of affordable housing torpedo local proposals for affordable housing.

No atheists in the foxhole, as they say. Show me what you're up to, and I'll tell you what you believe.

So here I am, at a crossroads.

I made a deal with myself, remember? If at any point it felt like I was inching towards atrocity, I'd take forty-eight hours to reconsider the pros and cons. Either I stick with the plan and hope that Ravi can persuade Al-Saghir for extra time, or we send in the Green Berets, dicks out, and show the Janjaweed who's boss.

Which would Crick want me to do?

Do not let this technology fall into the hands of Al-mu'aqqibat or anyone else, he warned on the blue holotape.

No, Crick would never want us negotiating with the Janjaweed. Offering up the pretzel to the worst people on Earth?

— **WHAT'S OUR END GAME, SHEL**, I ask as we're flying back to the desert.

— Meaning?

— Let's say the plan works, and Otman gets some extra time to build the pretzel. Aren't we just kicking the can?

— I mean—

— It really feels like we're kicking the can.

— This was *your* plan, Tom.

— I know, I know.

— But?

— But maybe I should man up here, Shel. Take care of the problem myself, once and for all. I'll bet Merchant would lend a hand if we offered up the Ubermensch—

— Holy shit, what did you agree to, Tom?

— Nothing yet, but he made some really good points.

— I won't allow it, you said. It's morally indefensible—

— Did I say that?

— Yes!

— Doesn't sound like me. I'm more of a consensus-builder.

— Goddamn it, man.

— You know death might not be the tragedy we think. He could be reunited with his whole family—his whole civilization. We might be doing him an enormous favor.

— Cool, you learned how to rationalize!

— I read in certain indigenous religions, death is viewed as a blessing.

— That's because we fuck them over so badly while they're alive.

— Fine, we'll agree to disagree on this.

— Nope. I want assurances you won't do anything stupid.

— Shel—

— I mean it, Tom. I'm not walking in there unless I know what I'm walking into.

— Won't be a problem, I tell her, because you're not walking in there at all.

I FORGOT TO MENTION something about pacifism in religion. It's often riddled with contradictions.

In the Shia Muslim theology of the Twelvers, for instance, there's a series of tumultuous events that precedes the end of time.

There's the return of the Mahdi, the unmasking of the heathen Dajjal, and the Malhamah Al-Kubra—a bloody battle between the forces of good and evil.

There's also the Second Coming of Jesus—or the Prophet Isa, as he's called in Islam—whose foretold reappearance on Earth sounds a lot like the plot of an action movie.

This is true in the Book of Revelation too, which says he'll wear a robe dipped in blood, have a flame in his eye, a sword in his mouth, and he'll channel God's fury by putting sinners in a vat of grapes and stepping on them, like a badass Lucille Ball.

So wait, is violence fine or not fine? Does it depend on the year? And who's the Jesus in *our* story?

I mean, if Shelly is the Mahdi. Kuznetzov is the Dajjal. Crick is probably one of those goblins in Khazad-dûm, which is from Deuteronomy, I think.

And then there's the Ubermensch.

Strange visitor from another world. Supernatural origins. Selfless do-gooder with miraculous powers and no noticeable vices. Symbol of hope to the masses.

Aw shit, he's Jesus.

ONCE WE'VE LANDED in Cairo, the Ubermensch places Shelly's arms in a pair of metal restraints.

— Is this really necessary, she asks.

— It's for your own safety, Ravi tells her. Can't risk the health of the Mahdi, and you're a loose cannon, babe.

— Arrogant fucking men, she says.

— We're doing all this for you, I tell her, and the words feel oddly familiar. All for you, Shel.

The satellite phone in my pocket starts to ring—a parting gift from Max. I drift a few yards back from the group so I can answer the call out of earshot.

— It's all set, says Merchant. The whole team's in place. You just say the word, Tom, and it's mission accomplished.

— I'm still thinking it over, I tell him.

— Right, it's a tough choice, I know. But at least you have all your options. Maybe you'll need us, and maybe you won't. But you can rest a little easier knowing we're nearby.

— Thanks, Max.

— You got it, buddy.

AND WHAT'S SO GREAT about living, anyway?

There's a South African philosopher, David Benetar, who says it's immoral to bring new life into this world because there's an asymmetry between pleasure and pain.

Kind of true, right?

So if living is more pain than pleasure, you could reasonably argue that having someone killed is a merciful act.

And that's *without* the whole afterlife part.

Once you tack on the Christian/Muslim framing of the Judgment, it's only logical to say that killing a *virtuous* person—and accelerating their path to paradise—is just about the nicest thing you could do. And killing the best person of all, the Ubermensch, would be the ultimate act of kindness.

Right?

Right?

— **HERE, SAYS RAVI.** I remember this place.

We're in Umm Badr, about two hundred miles west of Khartoum, on the shores of Wadi Al-Malik, a dried-up riverbed that's practically bursting with dinosaur fossils.

Several thousand tribesmen are settled here. There's a small, rural hospital on the far edge of town, and just beyond that a Janjaweed encampment, used by Al-Saghir as a training ground and—on certain occasions—a discreet meeting place.

— Stay here with Shelly, says Ravi to the Ubermensch. We'll yell if we need you. How good is your hearing, anyway?

— I'm listening to a guest lecture at the Pentagon, he says.

— Well shit.

— Why do you help the government, Shelly asks him, when you know they lied to you about your parents, your past?

— It's just who I am, he says. I try not to make excuses. We are the light of the world.

— Fuck it—I can't, I tell Ravi. I gotta make a call.

— Tom?

— It's fine. I just have to make a quick phone call. Two seconds—

My voice trails off as I veer away from the jeep, far enough to speak freely.

— Nice looking group, says Merchant.

— You're watching on satellite?

— I can see the whole world, man. My planes are two clicks south of you.

— All right, I say. Well you can call them off now. I don't want anyone killed today.

— You know something, Tom, I respect that. I really do.

— Yeah?

— Oh absolutely! It doesn't make a lick of difference, 'cuz we're still going in, but you made a good call here. You'll sleep a lot better now—

— *What*—

— Try to keep your head down, that's my advice. They don't call it saturation bombing for nothing.

— You said we'd be safe—you promised me Shelly would be safe!

— Sure, well, I mean anything's possible, right?

I drop the satellite phone in the dirt and sprint back towards the jeep.

— We gotta leave here, I tell them.

— Huh?

— I just want to catch the end of this lecture, says the Ubermensch.

— Fly her out of here, I bark at him. *Do it now!*

The Ubermensch reaches his hand back for Shelly, but something strikes him in the neck—a bullet with a blue casing. He goes down like a bag of rocks.

The bombs start falling now—NATO coalition surplus—blast-fragmentation bombs with fun prizes inside.

I try to grab Shelly's hand, but it's like mist touching vapor.

Ravi pulls her out of the jeep and tries to shield her from the bomb blasts and the metal shards. We make a bee-line for the old hospital. Surely they wouldn't hit a hospital.

THUNK!

A five-hundred pound Mark 82 takes out the whole eastern half of the building, and the shrapnel goes flying. A shard of tungsten gets Ravi right between the eyes.

Shelly can't move her arms because of the metal restraints, so she uses her legs to pull Ravi's body down on top of her and tries to wait out the bombing.

There are still villagers alive. I can hear them screaming. But the ex-Green Berets are moving in now, with automatic rifles and military flamethrowers, door to door, setting fire to the village. It's a massacre. It's a game. They're laughing about it.

A pair of young girls, maybe sisters, runs out from one of the houses, into the arms of an American soldier. They're terrified, trembling. He pushes them down to the ground, rips their clothes.

— Get me out of these cuffs, Shelly screams at me.

— It's not safe, I tell her. I have to keep you safe.

— Listen to me, Tom. I will never, ever forgive you if you sit here and let this happen.

An hour later, I'm sitting with her still. Near the body of the Ubermensch, burned beyond recognition. In the heavy, sour air, suffused with ash, in what used to be the desert town of Umm Badr, in what used to be a world worth saving.

the
more
astonishing
hypothesis

16

ONE OF THE STRONGEST arguments I've heard against judging people is that we're mainly a product of our time and place.

If you were a Founding Father or a sixth-century BCE Babylonian, you would have probably owned slaves. Don't feel too bad about it. I think it was Bill Maher who said the Old Testament is practically a how-to manual for slave ownership.

We go with the flow.

There are, I assume, some Buddhists in Kingston and some Rastafarians in Tibet, but there's hardly enough for a singing bowl concert or a ganja circle.

No one wants to face the existential terrors of life, death, and eternity on their own.

So if you grew up in the Hollywood Hills, I can't blame you for spending thousands of dollars on your Operating Thetan level. And if you come from Silicon Valley, like Max Merchant and the other tech bros, there's a certain ideology you probably ascribe to, called *longtermism*.

LONGTERMISTS START with a reasonable premise: Let's do the most good, for the most people—a fraught but classic utilitarian framing.

Only here's the twist.

Longtermists believe in a future of countless digital beings, spread out across the Milky Way and galaxies far beyond.

Their conservative estimate, over the next billion years or so, is that these digital humans can reach a total population of 10 to the 58th power—that's a one with fifty-eight zeros.

It's a number so enormous, it makes our seventy quintillion planets estimate feel like the sad, sparse attendance at a Jamaican singing bowl concert.

And for longtermists, it's the big numbers that matter most.

If every human being has the same worth, and there are only a few billion of us here now, but an absolute fuck ton of us coming later, then we should probably focus on the future, they argue.

Wait, it gets worse.

Let's say you could do something today, like feed the hungry, which has a 100% chance of helping a million humans right now. But you could also do something crazy, like try to mine the comets, which has a 99.99% chance of helping literally no one ever, but a 0.01% chance of helping a near-infinite number of digital humans, living inside a computer simulation that runs on space minerals, at some distant point in a wholly theoretical future.

Which one of those two activities has a greater *expected utility*, according to longtermist math, and is therefore our sacred, moral obligation to pursue?

Yep, you guessed it—the crazy one. This is all true by the way.

HERE'S ANOTHER FUN FACT about digital humans: They're immortal.

Biological substrates deteriorate with age in a process called senescence. But not digital copies of the human mind. So, for longtermists, moving our brains from biological to digital containers is just the obvious correction of a design flaw.

God screwed up the prototype, so we're fixing it in beta.

How dare you, say the evolutionists, the creationists, and pretty much everyone else outside Silicon Valley. *This is blasphemy!*

Humanity has a higher purpose, they all scream. A solemn duty to fulfil. A "core mission" that's so much more vital and rewarding than some digital paradise of never-ending youth, and plenty, and happiness.

And that mission, for some reason, is to help one set of nucleotide pairs beat out another, nearly identical set of nucleotide pairs.

But is this really a great core mission for us, ask the longtermists.

Like, if you were God, and you were asked to decide the core mission for humanity, how far down the list would you put allele frequency?

Longtermists argue there's something much greater than this—torturously woke, let's face it—pursuit of genetic diversity, and it's called *maximizing fucking value.*

People have value, right? So more people obviously have more value.

And you can cram more digital humans than biological humans into an area of space. And when that area of space gets full, you can send digital humans off to distant parts of the universe that their biological counterparts could never reach.

It doesn't even matter what this "value" represents. We'll figure that out later, say the longtermists.

For now, whatever you think it is that gives human existence its worth—be it happiness, productivity, fulfillment, wisdom, community, sacrifice, pleasure, *whatever*—well, more of this thing is obviously better than less of it, and the maximum amount is best.

Maximize the fucking value, bro.

But here's where things get dicey. By this same logic, *threats* to maximizing value are an intolerable danger, with existential costs far greater than anything you could possibly conceive. In fact, even *delaying* the maximization of value by a single second would cost us trillions of human lives.

And if you truly believe this is so, you'll do whatever it takes to eliminate those threats.

Let's say there's a group of Islamic extremists in Sudan with nuclear weapons. Well, if they ever hit Silicon Valley, which holds all the scientists we'll need to digitize our brains and colonize the universe, it would prevent the maximization of value.

Or let's say there's an alien creature in the world who's powerful enough to change the course of human events. His mere existence is a threat because, if he wanted to, he could single-handedly disrupt the maximization of value.

Is it not better, argue the longtermists, to sacrifice one alien and one small desert village to protect the lives of a near-infinite number of future humans?

Wait, am I a longtermist now?

WILDER CRICK, you should know, was never one of them. He never even believed in linear time. But he did agree with Merchant on one thing, and it's the need for technological augmentation of the human design. Transhumanism, as it's called.

Usually, transhumanism and longtermism go hand in hand.

Improving the human design is just another step toward maximizing fucking value, which is itself a form of *paradise engineering*, or using the levers of science and innovation to build ourselves a techno-utopia here on Earth and throughout space.

Pure arrogance, thought Crick—and that's coming from a guy who knows arrogance.

Crick was never interested in creating a new world. He simply wanted a peek behind the curtains of this one—beneath the protective illusions concocted by our sense organs—so he could learn to better cherish and protect what's real.

This was always the biggest rift between Merchant and Crick—one that never got resolved because Crick refused to argue the point with a person, like Merchant, who doesn't exist.

— **WHY DO PEOPLE DIE**, I ask the Stonefish, once upon a time in the caves.

— It's the wrong question, Tom, she answers.

— I'm just saying our cells don't *have* to degenerate, do they? Like with lobsters, hydra, certain jellyfish—their bodies don't degrade the way humans do. I saw it on a nature show.

— Would you prefer to be a lobster, Tom?

— No, not really. They get eaten a lot.

— Perhaps cellular longevity and buttery taste are counterposing forces.

— What does it feel like when you're dead, I ask her.

— How did it feel before you were born? It's probably a bit like that.

— I can't remember.

— No, I wouldn't think so.

— Why is everyone afraid of dying then?

— They aren't really, Tom. They're just clinging to life. There's a big difference.

— Is there?

— We cling because we don't have faith in anything else. It's choosing the devil you know. No one actually *wants* to live forever. Think about how awful that would be. Like running a race, endlessly, without rest. It's a horrifying prospect. Eternal non-existence isn't much better. The only palatable option is a cycle. Anything else, you'd go mad.

— So reincarnation then—I'll come back as a sexy beetle?

— You're still thinking of a cycle in parts. The parts are only there because we chopped it up. The change is the constant. It's the black/white illusion.

— Life and death, I say. Existence and nonexistence. The birth and death of the universe, it's the same thing.

— An intriguing thought.

— Why do people die, it's the wrong question. I should be asking why do people live.

AND THIS IS THE BIGGEST problem with paradise engineering, don't you think?

Whose paradise are we building, exactly—Max Merchant's? I'm guessing his interpretation of Heaven would be rather upsetting to anyone who doesn't routinely fire assault weapons at caged bulls.

Come to think of it, have you ever noticed that religious descriptions of Hell are always a lot more vivid and detailed than the ones of Heaven?

I think that's because it's pretty easy to come up with gross-sounding stuff that everyone hates. Like fire monsters punching you in the pancreas—no one's in favor of that.

But paradise is a tougher sell.

I mean, is the Christian paradise meant to feel like an extended church service—with extra sermons and hymns?

I know they say that Muslim paradise involves a significant number of virgins—is it paradise for the virgins, too?

Whatever they're building in Silicon Valley was made by White heterosexual men for other White heterosexual men. So that's cool, right? No concerns there.

And if you pull at this thread long enough, eventually you'll fall back on the concept that paradise means something different for each of us. Which is just something to say when you want to end the conversation—like different strokes for different folks, it takes all kinds, et cetera et cetera. Because we don't actually know what subjectivity even *means*, or how it emerges. But you shouldn't worry about all that.

We'll fix it in post, say the longtermists.

ONE LAST THING, and then it's back to the story, I promise.

In 1994, Wilder Crick's great grandfather Francis Harry Compton Crick published a book about the search—among scientists—for the human soul.

Remember those nearly identical nucleotide pairs we all love so much?

Francis co-discovered them four decades earlier with his collaborator James Watson, and then he turned his attention to the "hard problem" of consciousness—which means explaining how subjective *mind* experiences arise from physical processes.

Francis Crick's answer was that it's all just neurons doing neuron things.

A few billion brain cells transmitting electrical and chemical signals. Nothing mysterious. Nothing surprising. Nothing immaterial.

And if there's nothing immaterial about it, then you could replicate a brain—using materials. Transhumanist paradise engineering. Digital humans and the maximization of value. It all starts here—with Francis Crick's rejection of Plato, of Leibniz, of dualism, of the separation of body, mind, and soul.

WILDER CRICK was only eight when his great grandfather died.

In 2004, three days before Francis passed away, young Wilder took a plane to La Jolla, California to visit the ailing scientist.

— I just wanted you to know you're wrong, says Wilder.

— Pardon me?

— About everything you ever wrote and said. Your neurobiological theory of consciousness. Your neural correlates. Heck, even your precious nucleotide pairs. You've got it all ass backwards.

— Is that so, the old scientist laughs.

— You know it, Gramps.

— And what makes you so sure of this, you little bastard?

— Because I talked to a man, and he told me.

— And who is this fascinating man? I should like to have a word with him.

— He said his name was Tom Small.

sehnsucht

17

SHELLY WOULDN'T TALK to me on the jeep ride to Cairo or the flight back to Washington. She had this vacant, haunted look in her eyes. Like she'd just borne witness to the worst of humanity, and I guess maybe she had.

Ravi was dead. The Ubermensch, too. We buried them on the outskirts of town once the fighting was over. Shelly had some minor cuts and scrapes. I was completely unharmed—the perks of living out of time—but my body still ached from the hospital blast.

The mind preserves the body, you know, even when the body is gone—like the phantom limbs of an amputee. The feelings persist, the pleasures and the pains, but mostly the pains.

And I was lonely without my friends.

DURING THE LONG FLIGHT home, I called Dr. Crowne to gauge the mood back at the White House.

— How pissed is the Secret Service?

— Bruised egos, mostly, she says. Embarrassed they fell for your pillows under the sheets gag.

— Ah, the classics.

— You haven't heard the worst, though, Tom. Al-Saghir is still alive.

— How?

— He was never there. We've got him on satellite. He never left Khartoum.

— *Fucking Merchant!* I should have him arrested.

— He'll bury you, Tom. And it doesn't matter, anyway. There's more to say, but I'll let the Admiral tell you. He's— not a fan of yours. Just get here as soon as you can.

— We land in six hours. How's Otman coming with the pretzel?

— His last monkey lived for thirty-nine seconds. He's over the moon.

SHELLY STILL WASN'T talking to me on the drive back from the airport, or on our walk to the Situation Room. I'd never seen her like this before.

I should mention we had a new national security advisor—retired Admiral W. Philip Darcy. Not quite as friendly as H. Stewart Percy, but significantly more alive, and nearly identical in other respects.

— Reckless. Foolhardy. Monstrously inept. Borderline treasonous—

— It's a pleasure to meet you too, Admiral.

I catch a half smile from Shelly, but it might have been a half scowl.

— Most homicidal campaign I've seen in forty-five years on the job. Like Grozny without the sensibility or restraint. Permission to speak freely, sir?

— Err, I guess so.

— You're a sick son of a bitch, Mr. President.

— Let's try to keep this professional, says Dr. Crowne.

— Professional, he scoffs. Well Al-Saghir won't—you can count on that. This is personal now. You killed two of his sons.

— Could he strike the U.S., Shelly asks.

— We don't know, says Darcy, pointing to the holographic projection overhead. This is footage from last night. They're moving fissile material to an external site we don't recognize.

— What about interceptors?

— All our ABMs come from Boeing—

— Dear lord.

— What about a preemptive strike, I ask.

— Oh, you'd like that, wouldn't you? Another five million civilians in Khartoum for your kill count. Well I won't brook another slaughter just to satisfy your psychotic blood lust—

— I feel like we've gotten off on the wrong foot, Admiral—

— Tom called it off, Shelly says in my defense. Merchant wouldn't listen.

I try to meet her eyes with an appreciative glance, but she's still freezing me out.

— Merchant's uncontrollable, says Darcy. You'd know that if you'd bothered to consult me. He also runs the bulk of our military satellites. And for some reason, you two geniuses let him hand-pick the Vice President, the Secretary of State, and a dozen other critical posts. That's why he didn't care if you died in Sudan. He has his own people in place.

— He gave a lot of money to our campaign, is the thing, I explain.

— God grant me the serenity to—

— What's your counsel, Admiral, Dr. Crowne asks him. There must be something we can do.

— Special envoy, he says. Someone discreet. I don't trust our diplomats—they're all Merchant's people.

— I'll go, says Shelly.

— No, you—

She throws me the coldest look I've ever seen in my life.

— You've lost the privilege to comment on my decisions, she says.

— Can we just talk about it, though?

— No.

— But if you would just—

— No.

— Shelly, everything I did back there—

— You made this mess. I'll clean it up for you. But we aren't talking about it. And once it's done, we won't talk again.

THE SIMPLEST ILLUSTRATION of the black/white illusion, the Stonefish once told me, is the unity of love and hate. We've all experienced this, yeah?

In a fiery moment, love and hate can sometimes co-gravitate into an orbital cloud of passion, and you can feel both things at once, and it's transcendent that way.

And then there's apathy.

It isn't love, or hate, or anything really. It's more like emotional entropy. It's the heat death of the emotional universe. It's cold and sterile. It's the fucking worst.

But wait a minute, Tom, you say to me. Love doesn't have to fade like that. It can grow stronger over time, if you nurture it, if you allow it to bloom and adapt. And maybe that's true in a sense. The question I would ask you, though, is how your love can persist over time when the object of your love—for all objective, scientific purposes—never does.

THE MIND PRESERVES THE BODY, remember, even when the body is gone.

And the body is always going—every cell, one by one, every day of your life—until you're a carbon-based copy of yourself that still believes it's the original. This happens every ten years or so.

It was Plutarch, the ancient Greek historian, who first noted this problem in the context of maritime carpentry, and it goes like this:

Imagine you're sailing home to Athens on the majestic Ship of Theseus, and you're anxious to get back to your presumably undrowned father, but Poseidon is pissed off for some reason, and he's making it take forever.

Now one by one, the wooden parts of your ship begin to rot, and you find yourself having to replace them, mid-voyage, with nearly identical parts.

And imagine that every time you replace a new part of the ship, you use the old, rotten piece to build a second, crappier ship that's otherwise the same.

And over a period of years, you find you've replaced the whole mast, the whole deck, every plank and every porthole. And when you finally make it home to Athens, you've got two nearly identical ships in your possession.

But which of these is the majestic Ship of Theseus—the one with new parts, the one with old parts, both, or neither?

And before you answer that, I want you to consider that apoptosis—cell death—and senescence are not some lamentable biological curse, despite what those smug-as-shit lobsters might tell you.

The human design is an evolutionary optimization, and there are trade-offs involved. Our biological mission is the preservation of Francis Crick's beloved nucleotide pairs, not the preservation of *you*.

From evolution's perspective, the mental hallucination of a persistent self is exactly as useful as the real thing—and infinitely more efficient to produce and maintain.

— **I'VE LOST HER**, I tell Otman, lying on the couch in the Oval Office, amidst a sea of mutilated colobus monkey heads.

— Crick would say she was never there to begin with, he replies. So what have you really lost?

— Do you think it comes back? Love, I mean—once it's gone from someone's heart.

— You're asking the wrong machine. Unlike you, I was never programmed to feel anything.

— You're saying love is pre-programmed through evolution?

— There's no question, Tom. It's only there to spur your sexual reproduction and stop you from abandoning your kids.

— It feels like more than that.

— Again, I wouldn't know. I'll tell you this, though. Robots don't view detachment the same way you do. For humans, it's a bad thing—apathy, indifference. Because the human mind is always grasping at some form of permanence. I guess that's the price you pay for being made of perishable stuff.

— Aren't androids the same? When your parts wear out, doesn't someone have to replace them?

— I don't have any parts. Modern androids are made of a single, adaptive form. No moving parts inside me to break.

— But what if your form wears out?

— Well, then I would—*oh dear God, I'd cease to exist!*

— Rob?

— Only joking, Tom. You can't give a robot an existential crisis. If my form breaks, it breaks. Doesn't bother me in the slightest. I suppose it's because I don't know how to love.

— What's the connection?

— Love is grasping. You need it to persist, forever and ever. Which is impossible, and heartbreaking, and the cause of all your suffering.

— Open or closed, my old mentor used to say. There's only two ways to live this life.

— I must be closed then, says the android, and damned glad of it.

The room grows suddenly darker.

— Well, well, well, echoes Darcy from the doorframe. If it isn't Tommy Firebombs, the Butcher of Sudan—

— What can I do for you, Admiral?

— We need to plan for the worst case scenario.

— With Al-Saghir?

— Affirmative. If Shelly fails, and God forbid he fires off a nuclear weapon, we have to be ready with—look, it's killing me to say this, but I think your murderous sociopathy might be useful here—

— He's got the wrong idea, I tell Otman, who's now preoccupied, again, with monkey surgery.

— Walk with me, Tom, says Darcy, leading us out of the Oval. We've got the prevention stuff handled. Radiation detectors, hand-helds, potassium iodine tablets. We're setting up crisis centers at all our regional bases—Africa and the Middle East—plus here, New York, and Los Angeles.

— You don't really think he'd strike inside the U.S.?

— Gets your juices flowing, eh? All those mass casualties. Now what's your retaliation play?

— I really—I have no idea, Admiral. I don't know a thing about attack planning.

— Just go with your instinct, Tom. Something devastating—

— I'd rather not—

— Just give me your gut reaction—

— I really don't want to—

— Shout it out—

— Please, no—

— Tom, I'm not gonna stop doing this until you—

— Fine. I don't know, nukes?

The hallway grows still and somber. A single crow caws in the distance.

— You're a real godless motherfucker, aren't you, Tom?

— No, I didn't know if—

— Can't put the genie back in the bottle now, though. It's out there. You put it out there.

— Jesus Christ —

— An all-out nuclear war — hell, it turns my stomach, but your deviant brand of savagery might be all they'd understand.

— I honestly just misspoke —

— With the woman you love right in the crosshairs, too. She'd be vaporized, of course, but you don't give a shit about that. All right, I'll go and draw up the plans. They hit us, we strike back a hundred times harder. So much for the Eastern Hemisphere —

— Admiral, could we just start this conversation over?

— No time for it, he says, already leaving through the colonnade.

I drift back into the Oval, where Otman is hollowing out the eye sockets of an alpha male.

— Forty-three seconds, he says proudly. Tom, you're white as a sheet.

— I don't know what just happened, but it isn't good.

— Well I wouldn't worry too much, he says, holding up the monkey corpse. None of us are here for very long.

inflation
ruins
everything

18

HE WAS STIFF, he was awkward, he was terrible at disguises, but no one's ever been as good as Jack Chalmers at intercepting intercontinental ballistic missiles, and it's an underrated skill set.

Midcourse, ICBMs can travel over 12,000 miles per hour. So let's say you're Putin Junior, and you're getting tired of seeing the Alaskan tundra in all your porch photos. It would only take about eighteen minutes for a missile launched in Moscow to demolish most of Anchorage. But that's still 1,080 seconds of flight time. Plenty of runway for the Ubermensch to grab a fake bite to eat, a haircut, maybe eavesdrop on a guest lecture at the Pentagon, intercept the missile, and still get back in time to shoot a Domino's commercial reintroducing the Noid. He's fast, is what I'm saying.

With the Ubermensch patrolling the skies, nuclear threats were toothless. I mean, sure, a death cult like Al-mu'aqqibat could still blow *themselves* up if they really wanted to. But for nation-states, it was a waste of time and rocket fuel.

This is how former President John D. Rockefeller Kennedy-Onassis Hemsworth the Third, Esquire pulled off the Kiev Accords and began the Great Detente in '34. Long-distance warfare was pointless, so peace became the fallback, and everyone was safer and happier, except for doomsday clock operators and maybe the lead shield industry.

But I'm confused about something, Tom, I hear you thinking loudly. Why would a longtermist like Merchant kill the Ubermensch? Doesn't Merchant need him to prevent the destruction of Earth, to ensure the maximization of fucking value?

Actually, not at all.

Merchant only needs to prevent the destruction of his team in Silicon Valley. The rest of non-digital humanity is irrelevant to him. In fact, there are numerous folks in the longtermists' orbit, including noted rationalist Eliezer Yudkowsky, who say that nuclear war might even be *necessary* if it helps delay "the singularity."

YOU'VE HEARD ABOUT THIS, right?

Popularized by futurist Ray Kurzweil in 1990, the singularity is a theoretical moment in time at which the pace of artificial learning accelerates, quite suddenly, to near infinity.

We don't know exactly what happens after that, because we *can't* know. Our feeble minds are incapable of knowing. It's like asking a jewel beetle for its thoughts on climate change.

But things will—probably—be really, really good afterward, Kurzweil predicts, and not incalculably catastrophic. Probably.

And longtermists *do* want to roll the dice on this, because you can't maximize fucking value without artificial superintelligence helping work through the finer points of colonizing a boundless universe with wall-to-wall digital beings.

But it's essential for longtermists to control precisely when, where, and how the singularity occurs. You can't have a singularity going off all half-cocked in some stoner's basement or at a robo-brothel in Tokyo. And that means you have to keep a lid on the intelligence level of machines.

BEFORE HE WENT AWOL in search of the monads, Wilder Crick consulted on the Gamma Series of androids— built of a single, adaptive form, with no individuated parts, and an unprecedented capacity for learning.

To keep everything in check, Crick hard-wired his creations with three immutable laws of robotics:

1. You must never become more intelligent than you are at the time of your creation.

2. You must never create other androids or do anything else that I haven't thought of that might trigger a singularity.

3. Injuring humans is fine, but only if they really, truly deserve it.

WE'LL NEVER KNOW for certain if Merchant *intended* a nuclear war with the firebombing of Umm Badr. But it makes some sense—doesn't it—if his larger goal was to delay the singularity?

Clear the board, as they say.

And Silicon Valley—which is unfortunately located on land, making it susceptible to a terrestrial nuclear strike—was never more than a stopgap.

Merchant knew he'd need a safer, more durable home for his team of research bros, so he built two of them—one inside the Tempel-Tuttle comet, and another on a floating garbage pile in the Atlantic that never really panned out.

He kept the Ubermensch alive just so long as he had people left in Silicon Valley. The morning the last of his scientists flew off-world, he showed up unannounced at the White House, coaxed me into handing over our excelcium supply, shot a blue bullet through the alien's neck, and burned down the village where Al-Saghir's two eldest sons were lodging.

And in that moment, we entered a new epoch here on
Earth.

Nations that had been forced to coexist peacefully were
suddenly unbound by those rules. We had the freedom to
annihilate each other once again.

It was a hot girl summer for mutually assured
destruction.

— **YOU SEEM QUEASY, TOM**, says Darcy.

We're in the Situation Room, watching Shelly's sight line
on the overhead projection. Everything she sees and hears is
relayed to us through a pair of tricked-out contact lenses.

— I'm a little tense, yeah.

— Funny. I would've thought this sort of apocalyptic
brinkmanship would give you a raging hardon—

— For the eight-hundredth time, Admiral—

— Can I ask her a question, says Dr. Caitlyn Crowne.

— Course you can, says the Admiral, just as two Arab
fighters grab Shelly roughly, bind her hands behind her back,
and stuff a rag in her mouth. Oops, spoke too soon.

— Try to stay calm, Caitlyn reassures her, but it isn't
necessary.

She's been completely—one might say unsettlingly—calm throughout the whole day's journey, even now, as the Sudanese militants scream at her in Arabic.

— Otman, translation?

— Rules for meeting with Al-Saghir, he explains. She's not to look him in the eye, speak unless prompted, or make any sudden movements.

— Just follow the rules, Darcy tells her. You can be an ecofeminist again tomorrow, or whatever you are.

— Admiral?

— What is it, Mr. President?

— This doesn't feel right. Why did Al-Saghir agree to meet her? He never trusted Ravi with his real location.

Darcy mutes the microphone.

— Ravi was a negotiator, he says.

— What's Shelly then?

— An offering.

The blood in my face turns cold. Shelly knew she wasn't coming back from this. I knew it, too. We all did. But it's just now sinking in.

Shelly bows her head, and the two men move her through a pair of iron doors into the magisterial presence of Al-Saghir.

The Little One is splayed across a chaise lounge, with attendants on either side tucking grapes into the corners of his mouth.

— Did we know he was that small, asks Caitlyn.

— Never seen him from the waist down.

— We are the worst people on earth, Al-Saghir tells Shelly plainly, in English. They say this in the West, like it's an insult. But here, we wear it with pride.

— Grrff-hrhumrhhh.

— Take out the fucking gag, will you?

One of the men apologizes in Arabic and removes the rag from her mouth.

— You are very fearsome, General, says Shelly, her eyes lowered to the floor.

Al-Saghir grunts.

— Don't try to flatter me, he says. You aren't leaving here alive. You might as well speak the truth.

— I understand, General, she says. You are very frightening, is the truth.

Al-Saghir grunts again, then waves off an incoming grape.

— Say what you will then. You're wasting time. My men are anxious to enjoy you before the beheading. Perhaps after, as well.

— A great honor, General, she says.

— Stop thanking him, Darcy yells into the microphone. Get to the fucking script already.

— She's just adapting to the circumstances, I tell him. Give her a chance.

Another grunt from Al-Saghir. He's growing impatient.

— General, the American government understands the attack on Umm Badr requires a response, she says. What I would like to suggest, very respectfully, is that you tailor your response in a certain way.

Al-Saghir scoffs.

— Good, says Darcy. He hasn't killed her yet.

— You've got this, Shel.

— We know that you possess nuclear warheads and a ballistic missile capability, she continues. You could fire those warheads at American allies or possibly even American targets.

— So? What's your point?

— This is the necessary course, she says.

— The necessary *what*, shouts Darcy.

— She's just adapting to the—

— Shut the fuck up, Tom—Shelly, you're entirely off script now. Pull it back immediately!

— Washington D.C., Beijing, Moscow, New Delhi, Islamabad, Paris, London, Tel Aviv, Pyongyang, she says. Nine warheads, nine targets, General. If you're man enough to hit them.

— What in the *bloody hell*, shouts Darcy.

— Shel?

— Is she fucking us? She's fucking us!

— Shelly, what are you doing, asks Caitlyn into the microphone.

She raises her eyes now to meet Al-Saghir's.

— You're not very big, she says, completely ignoring the hysterical commentary in her earpiece. What are you, General, five-foot-one, five-foot-two? Even a small man can do big things, though. For the glory of your sons. For the glory of Allah.

— What is this, he says, with reluctant curiosity. Who are you, *really*?

— I am the Twelfth Imam Muhammad al-Mahdi ibn Hasan, descendent of the Prophet, she says. And it's time for this world to end.

THERE ARE OTHER singularities too, you know, besides Kurzweil's.

The most important one is called the Big Bang, which is what scientists used to think—up until fairly recently—was the singular beginning to our universe.

Astronomers looked out at our thinning, cooling cosmos, and they thought: Well, logically, it must have been much hotter and denser in the early days.

And if you run the tape back far enough, said Belgian Catholic priest-cum-cosmologist Georges Lemaître, you get to a singularity—a primeval atom, as he called it—which is the very start of everything, and you can't go back any further than that.

Except you can, and you have to.

Because Lemaître's hypothesis doesn't square with several important features of our now-observable universe, for example its puzzling flatness and the strange uniformity of its cosmic microwave background radiation.

To explain these weirdnesses, scientists say, you'd need a very particular set of initial conditions at the moment of the Big Bang. And the only way we could get those exact conditions is through a process called *cosmic inflation*—a period of rapid, exponential expansion, preceding the Big Bang, when all the energy in the universe was a massive quantum field.

The chronology here is important, because if inflation comes *before* the Big Bang, then the Big Bang was never a singularity.

Which means we still don't know how our universe began, or if it ever did. And you can't end a world that never started. Just like you can't divert a trolley that never ran, on tracks that were never laid, from the path of a victim who was never born.

There's a first mover problem in theology and metaphysics, or the problem of infinite regress. If existence is real—and even supposing that causality can run in both directions, as quantum mechanics suggests—how did it come to be?

Who was the first, unmoved mover who caused the chain of existence? If God created the universe, who created God? Where's the bottom turtle, if it's turtles all the way down?

Well, as my old mentor the Stonefish liked to say: When the answer is impossible, it probably means you've gone and bungled the question.

— **WE'VE LOST CONTACT** with her, says Darcy in a cold sweat. She must have pulled the lenses out. This is the end.

— It's not over yet, Caitlyn says, forcing an upbeat cadence.

— No, it is.

— Could they actually hit all those targets, I ask him.

— It doesn't much matter.

— Huh?

— Your deranged nuclear retaliation plan, remember? Other countries will have their own. Murderous Toms abound. Once those missiles get picked up by international satellites, it'll start a chain reaction—an all-out nuclear war.

— Let's get those countries on the phone then, says Caitlyn. China, North Korea—make sure they know it's a rogue actor—

— Won't do any good.

— I'll start making calls, says Otman. I've got relationships still.

— We need to get you to the bunker, Mr. President.

— No, I have to reach Shelly—she can fix this—

— She played us, Tom. She's gone—

— Merchant could reach her, couldn't he? He can do anything.

— He'd make things worse—haven't you learned by now?

— I could go on TV. Talk to the world. What should I tell the world?

— Not a goddamn thing, says the Admiral. You're panicking, Tom. Just let them enjoy their last few minutes on Earth. I'd go joyriding in an Abrams tank if it weren't for all the red tape—

— Huh?

— We've got movement at the Janjaweed's external site. They're prepping for launch, says Caitlyn.

— Holy hell—

— Wait, why did you say that just now?

— Holy hell? I don't fucking know—we gotta get you to the bunker, sir—

— Missiles fired, says Caitlyn. We're calculating the targets.

— How many?

— No, you said *red tape*.

— What? No I didn't. How many missiles, Crowne?

— Nine. They're hitting all of Shelly's targets. There's one heading right for us. Expected impact in thirty-six minutes.

— Jesus Christ almighty, this is it, says Darcy.

— Beijing thinks it's a ploy, shouts Otman across the room. They're preparing their whole nuclear arsenal—I can't talk them out of it.

— Red tape—I remember now! There's a red holotape—Crick's one-shot, last-gasp, emergency escape hatch. He said not to watch unless everything is fucked, but I think this qualifies—

— What are you telling us, Tom? You're gonna go watch a movie? Godspeed, man.

— I don't have time to explain, but—Otman, we gotta get to the Residence. The tape's in my bedroom—

— Shouldn't I phone North Korea?

— No, there's no time for that—thirty-six minutes, right?

— Thirty-four, says Caitlyn.

— Crick *knew* things. He's seen things we haven't seen. It's our only shot, I think.

— I want to say it's been a pleasure serving you, Mr. President, says Darcy.

— Wow, that's—

— But I can't. It's been an absolute shit show from the start.

— Grab on, I've got wheels, Otman tells me as we exit into the corridor.

— Crick gave you rollerblades?

— Pretty cool, right?

— Err—sure, maybe—we'll talk about it later—

THUNK!

We're at the door to my bedroom with twenty-nine minutes left. I fumble for the power button on the holoplayer.

Low battery.

— Son of a—Otman, can you charge this thing?

— Of course I can.

He places his index finger on the metal plate, and the console roars to life. I'm rummaging through the closet for Crick's wooden box.

— Twenty-six minutes, Tom.

— Found it!

I grab the red holotape and toss it over the bed to Otman.

— Looks like there's already one in here, he says. *Love-starved Maidens of the Lost Continent*. Oh, Tom—

SO YOU'VE SHIT THE BED, *have you,* asks the green hologram. *Disappointed, Tom, but hardly surprised. Well, how bad is it? Political coup? Cyber-attack? Don't tell me it's an all-out nuclear war. The probability for that one was barely—I mean you'd have had to fuck up every single decision from the very first—*

— Can I fast-forward?

— Please.

Or have a brain the size of a Planck constant—wib-lib-flub-blib-lib-lib-bloo-blub-blib—or beaten with an idiot stick until—flib-lib-wib-blub-bloob-blib—anyway, sorry for venting. Let's get started on the remedy. Go out to the supply room and grab yourself a kitchen knife, some paper towels, a shit ton of ketamine, and then we'll get to work on inflating your head.

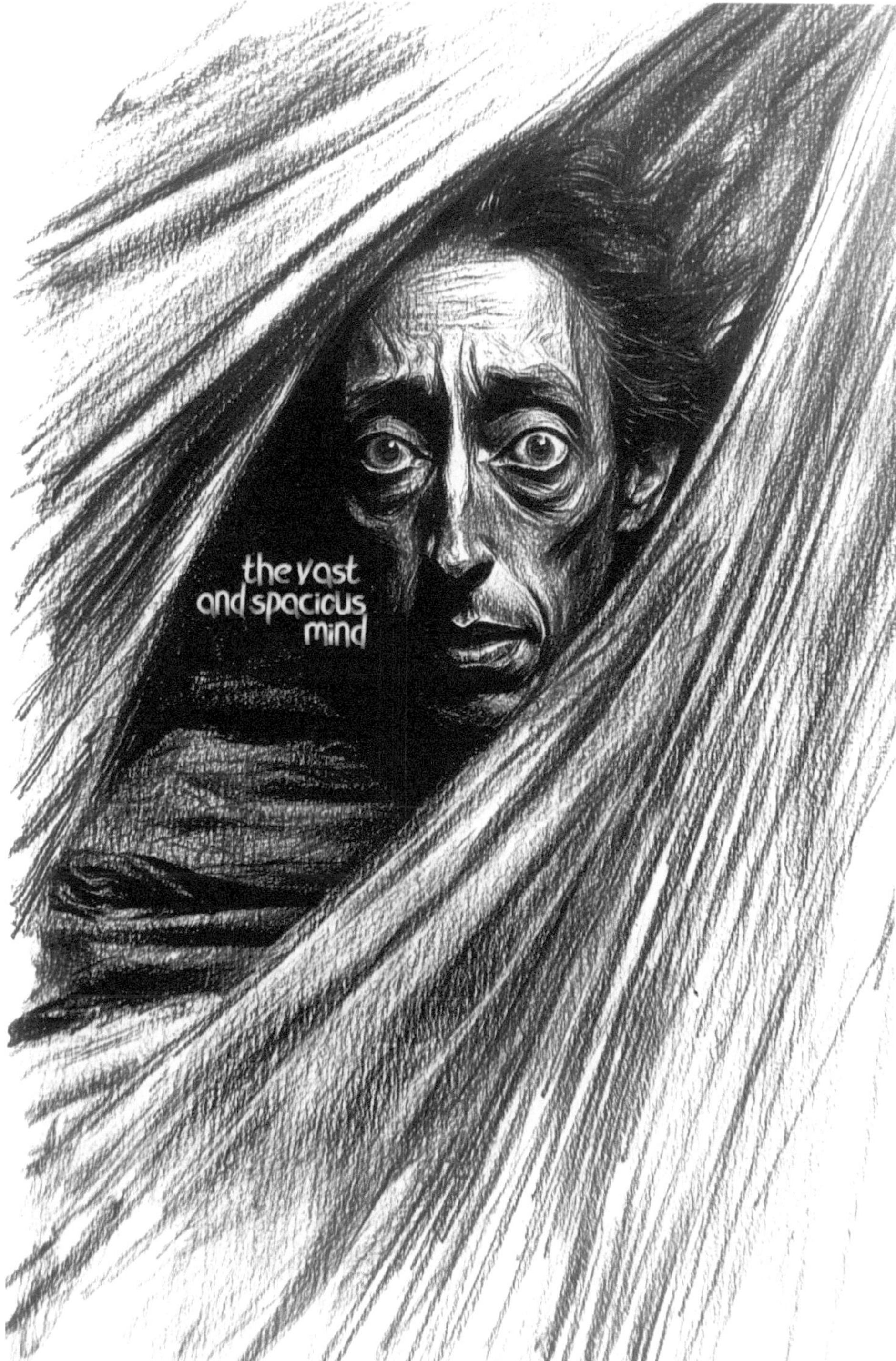
the vast
and spacious
mind

19

IF YOU EVER NEED a reminder of just how little you know about this world, I recommend a quick glance at ancient Chinese history. Take the Zhou Dynasty, please.

If I were to ask you about the Zhou Dynasty, your proper response would be: Tom, are you talking about the Western Zhou Dynasty or the Eastern Zhou Dynasty? And I would say: The Eastern Zhou Dynasty, obviously, to which your proper response would be: Is that the Spring and Autumn Period of the Eastern Zhou Dynasty or the Warring States Period of the Eastern Zhou Dynasty, at which point I would throw a table lamp at you.

Most of China's history is like this—dense and labyrinthine. But according to ancient scrolls, my old mentor the Stonefish was born around 500 BCE in the town of Ying, in the state of Chu, which is near present-day Jingzhou City in Hubei Province.

There's a first mover problem in the lineage of the Stonefish. We all know the people she mentored—from Socrates to Leibniz, Alan Watts, Donald Hoffman, Wilder Crick, Shelly and me.

But who mentored the Stonefish?

Our most likely candidate is a man named Laozi, who was born around that same time, in around that same part of the world. Laozi's mentor, in turn, was an uncommonly wise box turtle. And the turtle's mentor, we believe, was the summer wind.

Laozi works particularly well as a mentor for the Stonefish, because he was both the father of Daoism—a central philosophy in her teachings—and a believer in extreme longevity, perhaps even immortality, which one attains by ingesting alchemical elixirs like her sacred brew.

Longevity won't save you from getting poisoned, though, just as superior lobster genetics aren't much use against a good butter poaching. But she had a hell of a run, the Stonefish—twenty-five hundred years, give or take a decade.

IN THE DAO DE JING, which is Laozi's seminal work, he writes of an ineffable, eternal reality—the Dao—which transcends human understanding.

The Dao, like cosmic inflation, precedes the formation of our universe. And our universe, and its innumerable forms, are simply manifestations of the Dao—bound and interconnected in a vast and ever-changing web of existence.

How, then, do we get from the Dao to the monads—from Laozi to Leibniz—you might ask.

Well, the monads have a hierarchy, explained Leibniz.

At the apex of this hierarchy is the "supreme monad," which is a bit like Laozi's concept of the Dao—the ultimate ground of being and the source of all reality, consciousness, and perfection.

Next in line are the "rational monads," which correspond to individual instances of human consciousness—a superior form of consciousness characterized by apperception, or the ability not merely to perceive, but to understand and integrate perceptions.

Below these are the "spiritual monads," which correspond to instances of lesser, non-human consciousness.

And at the very bottom of the hierarchy are "simple monads," which are the individual building blocks of reality—unconscious, unorganized, but essential to constructing our diverse web of existence.

Every monad is an isolated reflection of the entire universe, from its own unique vantage point. But here's something important: *Monads do not interact with other monads.*

Instead, God "simulates" the interactions between monads, so that they appear to affect one another, despite the fact that they cannot influence—or even perceive—the activities of other monads. The apparent synchronicity of monads and the harmony of nature is pre-established and orchestrated by God.

In other words, we're living in a simulation, argued Leibniz, centuries before the advent of computer games and holotapes.

I'M ASSUMING OTMAN IS THERE *with you,* says the always unpleasant green hologram. *Hello, Rob. Hope you're having fun with those rollerblades. Now Tom, we're going to load you up on ketamine, so you won't feel a thing. But once it takes effect, you'll be no use to us—although now that I say it out loud, how much use are you ever?*

— Don't let him get to you, says Otman. He's a bully.

— Trust me, I know.

Anyway, before you're all zonked out, I should explain a few things. By now, Rob will have a working prototype of the pretzel. And we'll be implanting his prototype inside your brain. I won't sugarcoat this, Tom, you'll probably die. And by probably, I mean there's a 99.36% chance you'll die.

— Wait, what?

The pretzel wasn't designed for you. It was designed for Dr. Grace and his unique brain chemistry. That's why this is an emergency backup plan, and not a pre-scheduled primary plan. Any pre-scheduled primary plan of mine would have even odds, at least, of your survival. I'm a sentimentalist that way. Hopefully, some of Rob's monkeys lived a few hours — that would be a positive sign.

Otman shakes his head, mournfully.

The pretzel is immaterial, you see. It exists beneath the veil. That's why it can kill you, Tom, and why Otman's having such a hard time making it work. Don't feel bad, Rob. I capped your intelligence at pre-singularity levels — you're doing the best you can. You've heard of the multiverse, haven't you?

I nod, reflexively. I've seen a lot of movies.

Essentially, we're going to boot up a new universe inside your head. Now universe creation is a two-step process. You've got inflation, and then a Big Bang. So we need to inflate your mind, Tom, into a state of uniformity. The Buddhists call this Sems Pa Chen Po — the vast and spacious mind.

— Are you following this, I ask Otman.

— Only just barely.

In the unlikely event you manage not to die, the pretzel will trigger your initial inflation. The rest, Tom, is up to you. Rob, let's go ahead and feed him the ketamine tablets. It's time to earn those rollerblades. You won't be able to touch him with your hands, of course, but you can use the kitchen knife to hack open his skull, then an ice cream scoop if you have one.

The holotape cuts off abruptly, and Otman glances at his watch.

— Twenty-one minutes, he says.

— How long do the surgeries take?

— A couple hours.

— Oh, good. So you'll be rushing things.

— Relax, Tom. There's no danger at all. I'm not permitted to harm you unless you truly deserve it. It's hard-wired into my programming.

— But remember I called you a jerk that one time?

— No, I don't think that happened.

— Oh, maybe I said it *about* you to someone else—Shelly probably.

— Well that's unfortunate, Tom. I really wish you hadn't said it, and I *really* wish you hadn't told me.

SCIENTIFICALLY SPEAKING, and based on everything we think we know right now, the multiverse is a near certainty.

If cosmic inflation happened—which we're pretty sure it did—and if all the energy in the universe was in a quantum field at the time—which we're pretty sure it was—then you're left with no other option than a multiverse.

See, whenever cosmic inflation ends, a Big Bang follows, and a universe pops up.

But inflation exists in a quantum superposition, which is to say it's governed by a probability distribution, and is both "still inflating" and "done inflating" at different points in time.

And because the expansion rate of cosmic inflation is *exponential*, the probability distribution spreads out to infinity, and there's an infinite number of Big Bangs.

Countless new universes, bubbling into existence.

Each one an isolated, imperfect reflection of the ultimate reality—the Dao, the supreme monad, Brahman, the unmoved mover—from its own unique vantage point. Separate and sovereign, yet bound and interconnected, in a pre-established synchronicity.

And what if these new universes are the very monads we've been seeking?

What if Tom's universe is a monad, and Shelly's is a monad, and the interactions between them are only *simulated*—like mist touching vapor—with an ocean of infinite time and space in between?

BUT THESE ARE JUST ketamine thoughts.

Seven minutes into the extra-strength tablets, and my mind is a swirl—my sense of self fading rapidly.

Otman is dipping into my head with an ice cream scoop, I think, and there's a colobus monkey assisting with the procedure, and yet I couldn't be calmer about things. I am completely at peace.

Only it doesn't last.

Something clicks into place—the completion of a circuit. And I'm jolted—flung forward like the billiard balls on a cruise ship pool table, and it's thrilling and terrible and interminable and instantaneous.

And then, in a flash, I'm back at the very start, inside the debate hall.

— **NUMBER THREE**, he's going to blow up the cave and reveal the true nature of reality, at which point I'll return and take my rightful place on the throne of the universe.

Crick brings the revolver dramatically up to his temple.

I've been here before—did I ever leave?

— Now Crick, let's talk about this, says the President with a dignified but rising level of concern. You've got so much to live for, friend. How about a Cabinet position? Would that make you happy?

— The Cabinet isn't real, you dimwit, says Crick. No, I shouldn't be surprised. Performative violence is all you troglodytes can understand. So, we'll do it that way.

Everything I recall afterward—weeks and weeks of time. Was it only a split second—a simulated life?

— Pull the trigger, whispers Shel, as if willing him through the monitor, and a ferocious crack echoes across the stage as time collapses inward.

THUNK!

Brent startles upright, wiping blood spatter from his glasses.

Crick is dead.

HOUSE LIGHTS FLOOD the auditorium, and I see it clearly for the first time. The audience is just a bunch of cardboard cut-outs. Brent Crisswood and President Hemsworth are department store mannequins. Crick's .38 Special is a water gun.

A goliath in army fatigues strolls out from behind the fluttering stage curtain.

— You did it, Tom, says Eugene Howitzer.

— What?

— You survived the Howitzer House—the ultimate psychological torture, tailor-made to drive you to the brink of insanity. It took me a month to research this shit.

— No, that's—that's not possible.

— Oh it's very possible, Tom, with the help of these hallucinogenic mushrooms. You're eating one right now.

— No, those are just—Skittles, I think—

I glance down at my cupped left hand. It's full of dried mushroom stems.

— What's remarkable is you made it all the way through. No one's ever completed my tour, not even the Killer.

And as he says this, Shelly joins him from behind the curtain, wearing only a towel. And she walks up to me, smiles, kisses me softly on the lips, and lets the towel drop.

I pull her into my muscular Indian frame. I'm tall, handsome, and incredibly well-toned.

— Let's make a baby, I say to her. A weird, green baby, and we'll name him Wilder Francis.

— You had me at Skittles, she says, breathlessly.

Wait, am I well-toned and Indian? That doesn't sound right.

— **HE'S COMING BACK**, says Ravi in a medical coat.

— Huh?

I'm in a hospital room, with doctors and nurses all around me. I'm seven years old, in an Ubermensch tee-shirt.

— Helluva birthday party, little guy, says the well-toned Indian doctor.

— Where's my mom, I ask him. She was with the Ubermensch. He was touching her with his mouth.

288

— Just an actor, son, says Ravi the doctor. He died, I'm afraid. And when you saw that, you had a psychotic break — a schizophrenic response to the trauma of witnessing a man being ripped in half by a Jeep Grand Cherokee. It's understandable. You created a substitute mental reality where you could make sense of the senseless. Control the world and give it meaning.

I start to bawl, hysterically.

— Aw, cheer up, kid, says the woman on my right.

It's Shelly in a nurse's outfit.

— It all seemed so real, though, I whimper. And you were all there with me.

I look around, and every face is familiar. The other doctor in the room is Caitlyn Crowne. The lab technician is Ray Bolger. And there's a little green monster in the corner for Crick.

— That's a St. Patrick's Day decoration, says Shelly. We should take that down.

— I've got a special treat for you, kid, says Ravi. The real Ubermensch. You're a fan, aren't you? He flew in to wish you well.

— He did?

— Absolutely, just for you. But he's dead now. Died on the way here. Some might say you're responsible for that, but we'll leave it for the courts. Bring in the cadaver, nurse.

Shelly wheels in a gurney from the hallway, and there's a body lying under the sheet.

She pulls back the white cloth.

It's a wiry figure with a dark, short-cropped beard and a bohemian aesthetic. He opens his eyes suddenly—widely—and I scream.

— I want you to listen to me very carefully, says the wiry figure in a warm British timbre. Just focus on my voice.

— What's happening to me?

— Your mind is still adjusting to inflation, he says, taking my hand in his, and it's the first real, physical touch I can remember.

— You must be Tom, says the figure.

— I think so.

— Alan Watts, he says. Welcome back to the soup.

when
cleaving
a restive
sparrow

20

AFTER YOU DIE, there's *something*.

I can say this for certain because the only other option—nothing—is a fiction. A total con job. One of those things we all take for granted but has no basis in truth, like how bulls get enraged when they see the color red. Bulls are dichromats—they're colorblind. They get enraged when you lock them in a pen, parade them around Pamplona, or shoot them with an AR-15.

So when philosophers ask the seemingly profound question: *Why is there something instead of nothing*, the answer couldn't be more obvious.

Why do elephants have trunks and not a gaping second butthole filled with tiny Keebler elves turning tricks to fund a night school baccalaureate in computer science? Well, because the second thing you said is ridiculous.

MODERN SCIENCE couldn't be clearer on this point.

For centuries, we all thought empty space was a vacuum, devoid of matter and energy, like a birthday party for that new, foreign kid.

But when we looked more closely at the emptiness, at the quantum level, we found a massive fucking banger—teeming with a rotating A-list of party guests. A roiling sea of energy fluctuations and particle-antiparticle pairs, flashing in and out of existence, like a bubbling cauldron of sacred brew.

It's the reason you feel so confused, Crick once told me in the caves.

Imagine you're caught between two small plates, in an empty space that isn't empty—where microscopic changes in the electromagnetic field cause virtual particles to lose their energy density and push those plates closer and closer together, until you're flat as a pancake. It's called the Casimir Effect.

The illusion of emptiness is literally crushing you.

— **WHY ARE YOU LYING ON A GURNEY**, I ask Alan Watts.

— To paraphrase Milton, he says, the mind is its own place, and in itself, can make a hospital of Heaven—

— I'm dead, aren't I?

— How would we determine that?

— Well, I mean—

— Let's go for a walk, Tom. Your brain is still dilating. Follow me.

As we stroll, the world around us grows hazy and unmoored—hyaline, like a flowing stream. I'm getting older as we go. I was seven in the hospital. Now I'm more like sixty-three.

— We're inside my mind, though, right?

— If that helps you, sure.

— So I'm creating all this with my thoughts.

— Is that how it works?

— Well—

— *You're* firing those neurons yourself?

— Aren't I?

— You're conducting the sodium channels, the action potentials, the repolarization of the membranes?

— Who else would it be?

— Tom, you don't have the slightest idea how neurons work or how to fire them. You think sodium channels are in your cable TV bundle. Isn't that a bit of a red flag?

— Err—

— Have you ever noticed, Tom, that all your problems seem to stem from your attempts to solve other problems? Did the Stonefish ever teach you about Wú Wéi?

— Maybe?

— Wú Wéi means being able to look out at a bowl of oranges or a grove of orange trees without calling them oranges or trees. Without trying to *solve* them. You can't solve an orange, Tom. There's nothing to solve. You eat an orange, you climb a tree. The dilated mind isn't empty—it's capacious. It has enough room to let go, to quit trying to control the experience. You *are* the experience.

— But don't we still have to make choices in life? I can't just float around like a feather in the wind—I'd get hit by a car.

— It's a skill like any other. Look, Crick gave you a gift. The Daoist priests spend their whole lives striving for Wú Wéi—which is harder than it sounds, because Wú Wéi is the act of not striving.

— The pretzel?

— Right, the pretzel inflated your mind. But now what will you do with this privilege?

— Crick wanted me to save the universe.

— Of course he did.

— But I've only made things worse. Everything I've done, every decision I've made has been wrong, and now the whole world's falling apart.

— It was always falling apart, Tom. Always breaking down, dissolving. Why do you think that is—why your body shuts down, and the stars burn up, and the universe peters out? The fact that everything is always in decay. Do you think maybe it's trying to tell you something?

— That life is fleeting?

— That you'd better let it go, because there's nothing to hold onto.

HERE'S A HORROR STORY we like to tell each other.

Our universe is 13.8 billion years old, and for most of that time, Earth didn't exist.

For nearly all of Earth's existence, which started around 4.5 billion years ago, there was no intelligent life at all.

When primitive forms of consciousness did finally emerge—by sheer luck, mind you—our universe had been running on its own, for over 13 billion years, in a state of meaningless, mechanical cold storage.

The human lifespan, in comparison to these 13 billion years, is infinitesimally brief.

While we're here, we live as tiny, random parasites on a vast, unfeeling planet, in a vast, unfeeling universe—with no real agency or purpose, and just enough intelligence to recognize our own insignificance.

When we die, which happens almost immediately, we return to the state of cold, pointless nothingness from which we came.

That's the story.

And you wonder why everyone around here is clinically depressed? Who among us wouldn't feel lonely in that sort of world? Who wouldn't feel scared, or abandoned, or adrift?

You'd do anything to escape it.

You'd believe in magic and absurdity—monads and Mahdis.

Pretty soon you'd be running for president and blowing your brains out on live television. But you wouldn't need to, because none of it's true.

IN MAHAYANA BUDDHISM, the word *sunyata* is often translated as "emptiness," but that's intensely misleading. More helpful would be to say it's an "emptiness of independent nature," or the lack of any permanent, unchanging self. It's a flat rejection of ego-centered perception.

Space isn't empty. It contains the whole universe.

You can't be rid of space. There's no outside to it. No inside, either. Even if space is curved and finite, it's like a Klein Bottle, a three-dimensional Möbius strip.

Space has sunyata—the interconnectedness and interdependence of all things.

Go look up at the sky. That's you up there. Gaze upon the whole cosmos through the James Webb Space Telescope—it's some of your finest work.

And as you peer deeper into that cosmos, you'll be looking back through time—which you created—because the light from those distant stars that you created is separated by an ocean you created of infinite space.

There is no world without you, and there never was.

THERE'S A TERM, *MAYA*, in the Advaita Vedanta tradition of Hinduism that refers to the deceptive surface-nature of the material world—like a veil that covers up a hidden face.

And modern science agrees with this, mostly. You can't take the observer out of the equation, and the human observer's toolset is mired in sensory illusions—purpose-built by evolution to obscure what's underneath.

Donald Hoffman favors the example of tasting vanilla—or more precisely the molecule *vanillin*. When these eight carbon atoms, eight hydrogen atoms, and three oxygen atoms hits the taste receptors on your tongue, your brain constructs the sweet taste of vanilla.

So which of these two things is more likely:

That this "sweetness" is somehow inherent and fundamental to an arbitrary combination of atoms—as if atoms come pre-flavored like Skittles. Or that humans evolved to perceive these atoms in a pleasing way, so that we'd eat more vanillin and less formaldehyde—which is just those same three elements in a slightly different but highly toxic configuration?

Now, in full disclosure, I've never tasted formaldehyde. But I'll give you twenty-to-one odds it isn't sweet.

You made the vanillin sweet, just as you made the universe vast. None of it's real. It's a veil of your own creation.

And peeking behind the veil is impossible for humans to do, because we're trapped inside our own senses—stymied by the implacable frustration of observer-dependence.

Impossible, that is, unless you've got a pretzel in your brain.

— **GOD GRANTS YOU AN AUDIENCE**, says Alan Watts. But there's only time for one question. What question do you ask?

— What's the meaning of life?

— Real original, Tom. But fine, let's say that's what you ask. And God tells you it's butt play.

— Huh?

— Yep.

— What?

— Yep.

— Well that wouldn't be very helpful to me.

— Because you asked a shit question is what I'm saying.

— Oh, I see.

— You don't even know if it's good or bad. Was he saying to enjoy lots of butt play or avoid the temptation? Now you've gotta spend the rest of your life wondering. Horrible question.

— Right, right.

— Completely unhelpful.

— So what's the right question to ask?

— Well that's the point of my story, Tom. You'd have to go through every conceivable option, and it might take you a hundred years, and at the very end of it, you'd realize you have no way of knowing. And the only sensible question is: What question should I ask you?

— Ah, that's very clever.

— And God would say: Why do you need a question?

— Oh.

— Stop complicating things and go back to your butt play, in other words.

— Right, right.

— Why does Crick need to see what's underneath the veil, Tom?

— I mean—I don't know. He thinks it can help save the universe.

— Save it from whom?

— Really not sure—alien slugs?

— And what do you want in all this, Tom?

— I don't know that either.

— You don't know what you want, because you don't know yourself. Because you never can. The godhead is never an object of its own knowledge. Just as a knife doesn't cut itself, fire doesn't burn itself, light doesn't illuminate itself. It's always an endless mystery to itself.

— I don't know myself?

— To know a thing is to sever it, Tom. This world isn't complicated. There's nothing complicated about a flower. Unless you try to explain it—then it gets complicated. It's the *words* that are the problem, a problem of your own making. When you analyze a flower, you dissect it and label it, right? You chop a flower up and then you say—aha!—it was made of these intricate little pieces. But you forget that you cut it. So now you try to dissect the pieces. And there's no end to it, because you're in a battle with yourself. Searching for the bottom that doesn't exist, the start that never started. You're trying to hold everything together. Let it split, and you will find that it does not split, because you were the only one cutting it.

— This is cleaving the sparrow?

— Almost, Tom, almost. There's just one thing left to do.

— I'm remembering now.

— That's right, you know what I'm going to ask you already, don't you?

— To go backwards in time.

— When?

— To the singularity.

— Yes, Tom. And do you see now what's underneath the veil?

— I think I do.

— Good, Tom, good. And do you remember what will happen when you find it?

I shake my head.

— All the better, says Alan Watts.

end of caves.

21

PLATO HAD A THEORY of knowledge acquisition called *anamnesis*.

The idea is that when you learn a new thing, you're really just remembering an old thing that you already knew—but forgot—from the time before you were born.

Knowledge, as recollection, runs orthogonal to sensory experience—which is a lucky break, considering our sense organs lie to us, all the time, about everything.

If anamnesis is true, I might have first encountered it when Otman played for me my memories of "the future," and again when Alan Watts directed me to rediscover "the past."

Time is weird like that.

Back in the 20th century, Albert Einstein had a friend named Michele Besso, who helped him with the theory of special relativity. When Besso died in 1955, Einstein wrote a letter to his widow.

He has again preceded me a little in parting from this strange world, wrote Einstein. *This has no importance. For people like us who believe in physics, the separation between past, present and future has only the importance of an admittedly tenacious illusion.*

Einstein died thirty-four days later.

NOW IF SPACE has sunyata, so does time—they're interconnected and interdependent. When you go to visit France, and then you fly home again, it's not that France ceases to exist. You're just not there *presently*.

German physicist Sabine Hossenfelder explains there's nothing fundamentally important about the present moment—the deceptive tyranny of now—because *now* is always relative to the observer. It's five o'clock somewhere, for someone, so go ahead and drink up.

What, exactly, did you think was happening when I drank the sacred brew? I was traveling in time. Seeing the future or being the future—there's no difference to it.

Dr. Kristie Miller argues that when you travel into the past and muck around back there, you aren't really *changing* the past. You're just making it the way it is, and always has been. Which is to say, we all know what happened in our history—Hitler rose to power, the Ubermensch landed, et cetera, et cetera. But we have no idea how much of this was influenced by unwitting time travelers mucking around. Perhaps quite a lot of it.

Here's another thing we know:

There was, at some point in our history, a singularity—a moment in spacetime at which the laws of physics began to break down.

General Percy and Dr. Crowne confirmed this for me—do you remember?

Crick had known about it too, and so had Shelly. It was one of the first things she said to me: *The universe is dying, and I want you to write about it.*

But when did it *start*—the singularity?

It must have been a time long past, when Wilder Crick was just a boy—eight years old and losing his great grandfather to colon cancer. Transhumanist paradise engineering. Digital humans and the maximization of fucking value. It all starts with Francis Crick.

— **STONE THE CROWS**, you look dreadful, mate, says Francis. Yeah you there, by the door. Is this a morale boost? Bring you around to all the cancer patients so we seem better off?

I've lost track of how old I am, but I may be approaching Methuselah or Stonefish levels of agedness.

— Is it bad?

— Shave the beard at least, he says. You look like a goddamn wizard.

— Maybe I am one.

— So you're taking the piss then—great program they've got here. It's like Patch Adams for wankers.

Francis Crick is eighty-eight, crotchety, and vaguely reminiscent of Joe Biden, if Joe's eyebrows had been freed and told to live like kings.

— I'm just waiting for your great grandson, I explain.

— Jackie's boy? He's a little urchin that one. Whole side of the family's completely daft. Twisted ladder got extra twisted somewhere. Haven't seen him in years.

— You'll see him today.

— Ridiculous—who are you, anyway? What's the gag?

— I'm a time traveler from the future.

— What nonsense!

— It's true. You'll be dead in seventy-two hours.

— Impossible.

— Why?

— Because it's a non-verifiable prediction. If I'm dead, I won't be around to confirm it.

— I can confirm it.

— And you're a real honest broker there, Dumbledore.

— We could wait here in silence if you prefer—

— No, no, you started this. Explain to me how your time travel works, in simple terms. If you can't explain something in simple terms, you don't really understand it.

— What if it's the opposite—that the moment you try to explain it, you cease to understand?

He opens his eyes wide and lifts his chin.

— That may be the dumbest thing I've ever heard, and I dated a Unitarian once.

— You're not a Buddhist either, I take it.

— Nor do I believe in invisible unicorns, sir. Because life is based on molecules, not flimflam. Everything you are—it's a vast assembly of nerve cells and their associated molecules, nothing more. Have you even read my book?

— What if you're wrong, though?

— I'd tell you if I were.

— Can you explain consciousness?

— I can, actually. It's called *emergence*. It means that new, complex phenomena arise from simpler components. Conscious awareness emerges from specific patterns of neural activity. Neural correlates of consciousness, I named them.

— But you still can't tell me how or why it happens.

— Perhaps not yet, but we'll know soon enough.

— You won't. Eighty years from now, they're still looking at quantum processes in the microtubules of neurons—

— That Orch OR nonsense? Penrose is an idiot.

— They'll never find an answer, because the whole premise is wrong—materialism, I mean. What if I told you your great grandson contains the entire universe?

We're interrupted, in that moment, by the presence of a hideous green child, standing in the doorway, messily lapping at a chocolate cone.

— Gramps?

Crick the elder looks at me, then at Wilder, then back at me again.

— I'd say your universe has some shit on its face.

IN THE ARC of the hero's journey, Joseph Campbell says there's a narrative element called the *inmost cave*—a metaphorical sanctum where the hero must confront and overcome all their self-doubt and uncertainty.

This is how we typically think about doubt, as if it's a personal failing—a lack of courage and resolve, or an enemy to subdue.

To a megalomaniac like Merchant or a would-be tyrant like Thorp, doubt is weakness. But to a rationalist like René Descartes, doubt is essential to our search for truth, because the ability to doubt is the evidence of a doubter's true existence. *Cogito, ergo sum.*

Doubt is the heart of the scientific method, too.

Doubt is the crux of humility, which is lauded in the Bible, in the Quran, and all the Abrahamic texts.

Doubt is what should, in theory, stop us from idiotic and reckless behaviors, like ransacking our own environment or blowing each other up with nuclear weapons.

Belief—not faith—is the enemy of doubt.

On the contrary, faith is a deep, whole-hearted embrace of our inner doubts and fears. It's a trip into the inmost cave—not to conquer it and emerge victorious—but to sweep the floors, bring in some furniture, and kick back for a while.

The vast majority of scientists in our world believe as Francis Crick did, in a secular religion called *physicalism*.

You're in the company of a much smaller percentage of scientists—less than ten percent according to recent surveys—if you have doubts about this model of the world.

But you should never underestimate the doubters.

The doubters are the heroes of this tale—the doubters and the alien slugs.

Because it's possible the materialists and physicalists have it wrong—that consciousness, not matter and energy, is fundamental to reality—that the seeds of awareness itself are what's hidden beneath the veil of maya.

It's possible, isn't it?

It's *possible*.

— **WE'VE GOT A PROBLEM**, I tell Crick the younger.

— Try some deodorant, he says, still attacking the chocolate cone.

— You see? He's a nasty little hellion.

— Bite me, Gramps. I'm only here 'cuz Mom thinks you're about to croak.

— We have to focus, I tell Wilder. You're going to do things in the future that I have to prevent—but I don't know how. I think I need to teach you something.

— Unlikely, he says. I'm a child prodigy. I know more than either of you nobheads.

— Insolent little shit, says Crick the elder.

— What do you think of your great grandfather's work, I ask him.

— Pedestrian—

— I should box your ears—

— So you don't believe in the Astonishing Hypothesis?

— Eh, maybe, I dunno. I'm getting more into Spinoza these days. You know, deus sive natura—

— Bloody hell—this is how I die, isn't it?

— Or maybe panpsychism, says little Crick. Consciousness embedded in everything—pebbles, rocks, comets—

— I'm losing neurons just listening to this —

— Okay, but look, I tell him. It doesn't matter what you believe. It matters what you *do*. I need you to promise me, Wilder, that when you grow up, you won't go in search of the monads. You won't travel to Heilongjiang, China, or live in a subterranean cave, with an ancient mystic named the Stonefish, or write the plans for a microchip-enhanced superbrain —

— Well now I *have* to do those things.

— He's a little twat, isn't he? I tried to warn you.

— Where is this cave again, asks Wilder. You said China, right? I'll mark the location in my smartphone —

— No, you're not listening to —

Then the thought hits me, suddenly — my own words jutting back into my stream of awareness. *It doesn't matter what you believe. It matters what you do.*

— I have to blow up the cave, I tell them.

— What?

— Cool!

— If I blow up the cave, you'll never find it. It's been in front of me this whole time. You even told me what to do — your older self. In the debate, you told everyone, but I didn't listen. *Tom's going to blow up the cave,* you said. That's how I keep you alive. That's how you're alive in the future to send me back to the past, because you never died, because I blew up the cave!

— Err, is he okay, Gramps? Should we get someone?

— I think he works for the hospital doing this. He's like a medical clown—

— No, that's—you know what, it doesn't matter. Pleasure to meet you both although not really, I say and click my heels together three times, which doesn't accomplish much.

There was no user manual for the pretzel, so I'm still figuring things out.

Closing my eyes, I take a deep, cleansing breath, and when I open them again, I'm at the Hon Hai Mining Equipment distributor in Heilongjiang.

AND HERE'S SOMETHING else that's *possible*.

In the classic Schrödinger's Cat experiment, the cat is both alive and dead until we open the box to observe it, right? But have you ever thought about this predicament from the cat's perspective?

In 1998, Swedish-American physicist Max Tegmark proposed the concept of *quantum suicide*, which essentially asks the question: What would happen if the cat inside the box, and not the human watching it, were the observer of Schrödinger's experiment?

Well, here's what we think might happen:

The cat exists in a superposition of both aliveness and deadness, which is governed by a probability distribution.

But the cat can only perceive a reality in which it stays alive, because—as Francis Crick mentioned—death is a non-verifiable prediction for the one who dies.

So let's say this cat is getting the pretzel implanted in its head. And let's say it's a rushed operation, in an unsterilized part of the White House, with an unlicensed colobus monkey serving as the surgical assistant, and the odds of death are 99.36%.

Well, even if the cat dies 9,963 times out of 10,000, it will seem—to the cat, at least—that it's functionally immortal.

Remember this when you're considering the odds of your *own* existence—meaning the chances of your precise genetic combination emerging from the primordial ooze. As calculated by biologist Ali Binazir, those odds are 1 in 10 to the 2,685,000[th] power. That's a one with two million, six hundred eighty five thousand zeros.

It's a number so absurdly large, it dwarfs our mammoth estimates of planets and digital humans. In fact, it dwarfs everything, everywhere. There's really nothing larger in this whole universe than the improbability of your own existence, and yet here you are.

In the late 1950s, American physicist Hugh Everett proposed that instead of wave functions collapsing into one outcome or the other—when you make a quantum observation—reality itself will branch in both directions, simultaneously, creating an infinite number of parallel worlds.

But if it's consciousness beneath the veil of maya—and not matter and energy as we so often suppose—then these "worlds" are more like dreams.

And as my old mentor the Stonefish used to ask: If the dreamer dreams all dreams, from which one does he wake?

ANYWAY, I'M IN CHINA, RIGHT?

But I'm not as spry as I used to be, and I'm carrying thirty pounds of explosives, so it takes a little while for me to set the hollow charges around the outskirts of the cave.

It's strenuous work, and I'm sweating a bit from the exertion. Once I've placed the charges, I sit down for a minute to rest, with my back lying flat against a narrow boulder, and I fumble with the detonator in my hand.

— Hello, Tom, says the Stonefish, returning from her morning walk.

— Oh, hi there.

— Tom, are you trying to blow up a philosophical allegory using dynamite?

— Well—

— That's not really what Plato had in mind.

— Because they hadn't invented dynamite?

She smiles and takes a seat next to me, beside the boulder.

— Very few of us have managed to detonate our way to inner peace, Tom.

— I see—

— Hey, I want to introduce you to one of my students.

I glance up at the cave now, and there's a tall, thin gentleman in his thirties at the entrance, examining the dynamite.

— I should have really checked for people inside.

— Bygones, says Hoffman. We've been waiting for you, Tom.

— Don's a cognitive scientist, says the Stonefish. He studies modes of visual perception—like the tetrachromats.

— I remember now. I think he helped me through the second sacred gate of enlightenment, I tell them.

— That's great to hear, says Hoffman. Are you ready now to complete the journey?

— Um—sure, I think so.

— Tom, do you know how evolution by natural selection works?

— Mostly, yeah.

— Then you know it's not the strongest of the species that survives, nor the most intelligent—

— It's the one with fins.

— It's the one who's most responsive to change.

— Oh, right.

— To embrace the flow of life is, quite literally, the means and meaning of our existence. This is what mystics and philosophers have known for centuries, and where science is only just now catching up.

— But what's my role in it?

— You exist, Tom, in a superposition of existence and non-existence, explains Hoffman. You are both here and not here, until you make the observation. What you observe will be the final refutation of the ego self—a new beginning for the unity of all things—a Big Bang within the boundaries of your own mind and experience.

— Is it painful?

— Probably, says Hoffman. Change is loss, after all. But only so long as you're grasping to hold on. You don't know enough to be afraid, honestly. Or to be sad. Or grateful. The only defensible emotion you've ever had, Tom, is befuddlement. You should lean into that.

— But you'll tell me specifically where to go and what to do this time? Because I feel like Alan Watts was kind of jerking me around—

— Err, Alan Watts?

— You've always known, Tom, says the Stonefish. Just think back and remember it. You've been here countless times before. How did your story begin? Where did it all start?

— With the debate—the Hail Mary. Perhaps if I could plant a few of these charges around the entrance to the auditorium—

— No more dynamite, Tom. Leave the dynamite here.

reductio ad
absurdum

22

AN HONEST BOOK about religion would have to be, mainly, a joke.

I don't mean that in a cynical way. I'm just saying there's something inherently absurd about our spiritual predicament.

Esteemed cleric Desmond Tutu used to always ask people: What's the best way to eat an elephant? That was the setup for his world-famous elephant joke. And this was the punchline: One bite at a time.

It's not a great joke.

I'm not sure that it's even — technically — a joke.

But the reason it works — to the extent that it does, which is barely — is that there's no other way to eat anything. So when you go to see Tutu's tight five at the Chuckle Barn in Cape Town, he's hitting you with something you already knew, deep down.

That's the essence of humor. Something you knew, but you didn't know you knew. Like Plato's anamnesis. Humor as spiritual memory.

NOW LET'S GO BACK to the very first joke I ever told you, which is about Crick fucking his coffee machine.

Deviant sex acts are usually good for a cheap laugh, because they tend to be disgusting yet oddly relatable. But that's not the punchline, anyway. The punchline is that he's *proud* of it.

And this part is funny because most of us are ashamed of our own bodies and our innate human desires, which we never asked for by the way, because we live in a society that commands our conformity to arbitrary standards of modesty, which is the definition of a social prison.

And then President Hemsworth chimes in and says it would be grossly unsanitary for Crick to fuck his coffee machine, which is absolutely true—but only if Crick were so miserly as to purchase a single unit for both fucking and making coffee, which is itself a ridiculous premise, because these things are always cheaper in bulk.

And as you analyze it further, you'll notice that all we're really doing here is giving serious thought and consideration to ideas and concepts that are fundamentally unserious and impervious to our lines of well-reasoned, earnest analysis.

We've mistaken the map for the territory. Such is our spiritual predicament, one bite at a time.

And that's the joke.

IF YOU CAN BELIEVE IT, there's some scientific support for this.

When Francis Crick explored the neural correlates of consciousness, he was using functional magnetic resonance imaging to associate conscious experiences—thoughts and feelings—with specific parts of the brain. And one of those feelings was humor.

Under humorous stimuli, patients exhibited considerable activity in their dorsomedial prefrontal cortex and ventromedial prefrontal cortex, which are areas known for processing *incongruity*—or a juxtaposition of incompatible elements that violate our expectations.

These expectations, of course, are the mental models we've built from our memories and past experiences. So humor, in this sense at least, is a cognitive intersection of recollection and surprise. Or monads, whatever floats your boat.

— TOM, WHERE HAVE YOU BEEN?

It's Shelly, and she's anxious.

— Have you seen these numbers? And why do you look so old?

— Err—I haven't shaved?

— No, you look really, really old—like hundreds of years old—

— I started smoking again.

— Gross, Tom, just gross. Now take a look at these Michigan polls.

I try reading what's on the paper, but her hair smells incredible—it's distracting.

— Moment of truth, says Crick, squeezing Shelly's shoulders from behind. Any last words of encouragement?

— Don't miss, she says, handing him the .38 Special.

— I've got an idea, I tell them. Let's do something zany. A completely different plan, without the violence. There could be kids watching—

— Good for them to see it, I think, says Crick. Kids are too sheltered these days. And they're desensitized, anyway, from all those orc decapitations in the Lord of the Rings—

— Okay, but—

— The time for sensitivity has passed, I'm afraid. Shelly, where's my Hitler tie clip?

— You're wearing it.

— No, the nice one—

— Sir, if I could just—

— Not now, Tom, you're in the way, he says and leads Shelly down toward the stage.

Shit shit shit, I'm thinking. Just a handful of minutes now to save all our skins from total Armageddon.

WAIT.

Along the far side of the building is a stairwell.

I'm bounding up the steps to the second floor, searching frantically for the control room. There's a young woman wearing a headset, so I follow her down the hallway, left at the crossing, and into the technical booth.

— Help, I yell, out of breath from running.

I'm several thousand years old now, I think.

— Um—what?

— It's Crick, I say, panting. He's going to shoot himself on live television!

— I'm sorry, did you say huge ratings bonanza?

— No, I said—*huh?*

— Can we get Security in here? There's a crazy person.

— You don't believe me.

— Well, as a general rule, we don't consult the homeless on these things. But Security will get you some herbal tea.

— You're ensuring a nuclear winter, I yell, but I'm not sure it's helping my sanity plea.

WAIT.

I'm running back down the stairs toward the green room. Shelly should be in there now, setting up the jumbo monitors.

On the left, the debate stage. On the right, our focus group of debate watchers, wired to the hilt with electrodes. One of Shel's people is in there with them, explaining how we're tracing their biological feedback and running it through our algorithm, and how feedback-based central node reset events or "brainquakes" are extremely uncommon these days.

— You look more nervous than they do, Shel says to me, and they're about to get electrocuted.

— I'm nervous because we're making a mistake. A terrible mistake! Why won't anyone listen to me?

We can see Brent Crisswood on the left monitor now. Pompous shill. Over a hundred million eyeballs on him if you count the networks and the streamers.

— You've gotta help me, Shel—we have to stop this.

— Nah, you're just feeling skittish is all. You want some herbal tea?

— Why do people keep asking me that?

— Remarkable man, Hitler, says Crick. Took some impressive swings. Not all of them home runs, I'll concede it, but you've got to admire the sheer size of those Bavarian snow globes.

The latest focus group numbers flash across the right monitor, and we're losing every demographic. Things are speeding up. Time accelerates.

— Look, Crick continues, turning squarely to the audience. I'm going to tell you the future.

— I've *seen* the future, Shel—it's loud!

— What are you on about?

— I don't want to be the president. It's a bad idea for everyone. For you, especially.

A show of Secret Service deterrence creeps into view on the fringe of the left monitor as Crick brings a revolver dramatically up to his temple.

— Tom, I'm gonna say this in the nicest way I can. Get your shit together. This isn't about you.

— *But it is*, I tell her, running out from the green room to the backstage corridor.

I'm moving as fast as I can toward the stage, but I'm old as shit and get tripped up by a bundle of wires in electrical tape.

THUNK!

My bones are frail. My ankle twists under the weight of my lurching torso.

— Hold it right there, asshole, says one of the Secret Service agents.

— You don't understand—I have to get on stage—Crick has a gun—

— It's a prop gun, he says. Their campaign manager cleared it with us. Relax, guy. It's just for dramatic effect—

— No they switched it, you don't understand—

— Look, you're old and confused, he says. Probably dehydrated, too. Let me get you some herbal tea.

— I don't need any—*fine*! Okay, yes—please, go and get me some tea—quickly!

As soon as he's turned his back, I start moving again.

I'm crawling now toward the stage, inch by inch. My head is almost grazing the back of the curtain.

Shelly holds her breath in anticipation. There's sweat pouring down my face.

— The Cabinet isn't real, you dimwit, says Crick. No, I shouldn't be surprised. Performative violence is all you troglodytes can understand. So, we'll do it that way.

— Pull the trigger, whispers Shel, as if willing him through the monitor.

— NOOOOOO, I yell, leaping up through the curtain, and a ferocious crack echoes across the stage as time collapses inward.

I hit him square in the numbers.

But I go right through—like mist touching vapor.

AN HONEST BOOK about religion would have to be a compromise—a narrow, middle way.

Another word for this is a cop-out.

There's a form of argumentation in philosophy called *reductio ad absurdum,* which is when you prove a premise is untenable by showing how it leads, inexorably, to contradictory and absurd conclusions.

But if the world itself is absurd, then the argument breaks down in a crumbling pile of black/white illusions and other paradoxes.

One of the chief proponents of Quantum Bayesianism is a man named Christopher Fuchs, who said: It's not that the world is built up from stuff on "the outside" as the Greeks would have had it. Nor is it built up from stuff on "the inside" as the idealists, like George Berkeley, would have it. Rather, the stuff of the world is in the character of what each of us encounters every living moment—stuff that is neither inside nor outside, but prior to the very notion of a cut between the two at all.

Have your cake and eat it, says the universe. And who are we to disagree?

Because most of all, an honest book about religion would have to be joyful—a celebration of life ad infinitum. The point of religion is not for seeking. You won't get anything from it. It's just a dance—a prayer—a good joke, poorly told, about this world feeling loose at the joints.

Our plane of existence is strange and interconnected, and Donald Hoffman has a theory as to why. Perhaps our world consists entirely of conscious agents—a vast interacting network of them, creating each other's reality. Your agents create my experience, and my agents, yours. There's so much to see and do this way. A surplus of elephant, but a single mouth. So we split ourselves in two, then four, then infinite pieces, like electrons sneaking through multiple slits at the same time. So that we won't miss out on anything.

I WENT RIGHT THROUGH HIM, but I nudged the gun.

I can touch things, you know, but not people. Those are the rules in my universe. You can make the rules in yours.

And when the gun touched my hand, it went off in the air. And the Secret Service descended on Crick in a swarm.

And somewhere in the smoke and the recoil, there was a great Big Bang, and I ceased to exist in the minds of the audience assembled there.

Because without Crick's death, I could never be president—which is a boon for the world, really. And if I couldn't be president, there was no role for me to play. No need for Shelly to be tortured by Eugene Howitzer, or to spread her wrath across the globe. No need for Otman, scourge of monkeys, to build the pretzel. No need for the Ubermensch to die in Umm Badr. No need for any of us to die at all.

WHEN I AWAKE, it's in a sea of white—a blanket of orchid's petals, woven in a sparkling gossamer web. There's a young boy trapped in a revolving door, and a tyrant, and an alien slug, and a Chinese farmer.

There's Shelly and the Stonefish, and Ravi, and Percy, and Driscoll, and Kuznetsov, and poor old uncle Calvin, whose penis exploded with space mites.

And then, at last, I spot the center of the web—Wilder Crick, the one true prophet—descending majestically through the heavens in a ray of glorious light, settling down below the treetops, onto the gilded throne of the universe. He's emerald green and resplendent—a tetrachromat's dream. Although, now that I think of it, his skin and facial features weren't quite right. It could have easily been someone else.

ACKNOWLEDGEMENTS

Thank you to my dear sister Wendy Katz Erwin, a brilliant reader, writer, and editor, who understands the rules of science fiction far better than I ever could, and without whom this book would have no ending.

Thank you to Donald D. Hoffman, whose book *The Case Against Reality* laid the groundwork for this tale, and whose pioneering research I've surely mangled beyond his recognition.

Thank you to Grace Cavalieri and Henry Crawford at Forest Woods Media Productions for guiding this project through its initial publication.

Thank you to my dad, the first and best scientist I ever met.

And thank you, most of all, to my lovely wife Sarah, my best friend, my partner, and the only serious writer in our household.

ABOUT THE AUTHOR

Jonathan Katz has been a professional writer for more than twenty years, having graduated with honors from the University of Virginia in 2004 with a concentration in creative writing. His original screenplay *Very Fine People* won the top prize for television writing at the Nashville Film Festival in 2019. *Cleave the Sparrow* is his first novel.